PRAISE FOR DIXIE BROWNING

"There is no one writing romance today who touches the heart and tickles the ribs like Dixie Browning. The people in her books are as warm as a sunbeam and just as lovely."

—Nora Roberts

"Dixie Browning has given the romance industry years of love and laughter in her wonderful books, stories that were sometimes serious, sometimes whimsical. She has also given of herself, out of a boundless warmth and generosity. Her fiftieth romance should be golden, just like the lady herself."

—Linda Howard

"A true pioneer in romance fiction, the delightful Dixie Browning is a reader's most precious treasure, a constant source of outstanding entertainment."

—Melinda Helfer, *Romantic Times*

"Dixie's books never disappoint—they always lift your spirits!"

—Mary Lynn Baxter

"Dixie Browning is a warm, wonderful, classy lady with a great sense of humor. And it shows on every page in every book she has written."

—Suzanne Simms

"Each of Dixie's books is a keeper guaranteed to warm the heart and delight the senses. Congratulations, Dixie, on your fiftieth romance!"

—Jayne Ann Krentz

Dear Reader,

You know, there are some months here at Silhouette Desire that I feel are simply perfect! Naturally, I think each and every Desire book is just wonderful, but occasionally the entire lineup is so special I have to mention each book separately.

Let's start with *Hazards of the Heart* by Dixie Browning. This talented author has been writing for the line since nearly the very beginning—over ten years ago! Still, it's hard for me to believe that this is her *fiftieth* Silhouette book. *Hazards of the Heart* is highlighted as our *Man of the Month,* and it also contains a special letter from Dixie to you, her loyal readers.

Joan Johnston is fast becoming a favorite, but if you haven't yet experienced her sexy western-flavored stories, please give her a try! *The Rancher and the Runaway Bride* is the first of her new series, *Hawk's Way,* which takes place—mostly—on a Texas ranch. The stories concern the lives—and new loves—of the two Whitelaw brothers and their sassy sister.

A book from Lass Small is always a delight, and this time around we have *A Disruptive Influence.* What—or *who?*— is this disruptive influence? Why, read and find out.

As far as I'm concerned, Nancy Martin has been too long from the list, therefore I'm *thrilled* with *Good Golly, Miss Molly.* Doreen Owens Malek is another author we just don't see enough of, so I'm equally excited about *The Harder They Fall.* And I love Lucy Gordon's emotional writing style. If you're also a fan, don't miss *Married in Haste.*

Six spectacular books by six dynamite authors. Can you ask for anything more?

Until next month, happy reading!

Lucia Macro
Senior Editor

DIXIE BROWNING
HAZARDS OF THE HEART

SILHOUETTE *Desire*®

Published by Silhouette Books New York

America's Publisher of Contemporary Romance

SILHOUETTE BOOKS
300 East 42nd St., New York, N.Y. 10017

HAZARDS OF THE HEART

Copyright © 1993 by Dixie Browning

All rights reserved. Except for use in any review, the reproduction or utilization of this work in whole or in part in any form by any electronic, mechanical or other means, now known or hereafter invented, including xerography, photocopying and recording, or in any information storage or retrieval system, is forbidden without the permission of the publisher, Silhouette Books, 300 E. 42nd St., New York, N.Y. 10017

ISBN: 0-373-05780-6

First Silhouette Books printing April 1993

All the characters in this book have no existence outside the imagination of the author and have no relation whatsoever to anyone bearing the same name or names. They are not even distantly inspired by any individual known or unknown to the author, and all incidents are pure invention.

® and ™:Trademarks used with authorization. Trademarks indicated with ® are registered in the United States Patent and Trademark Office, the Canada Trade Mark Office and in other countries.

Printed in the U.S.A.

Books by Dixie Browning

DIXIE BROWNING

is celebrating her fiftieth story for Silhouette Books
with the publication of this book. A reader favorite for
over a decade, Ms. Browning was in the second month
of Silhouette Romance's launch and has contributed
to numerous special projects, promotions and reissues. Thank you, Dixie!

Prologue

Jake had been watching the blonde with the big front deck for some time now. He didn't know why, exactly. She wasn't the most beautiful woman in the room by any stretch of the imagination. Maybe it was the fact that a guy didn't see too many pregnant women at these bashes. Not all *that* pregnant, at least. She looked about twelve months gone.

His gaze moved around her table. He had recognized two of the four people there. Charles Alderholt had run for governor in the past two elections. Old Charlie ought to know better than to wrap a fifty-inch belly in a tartan cummerbund. Hell, he looked even more pregnant than the blonde.

Sitting at the same table, with some bleary-eyed bimbo practically jumping his bones, was Walt Porter. Old Raleigh family. Jake knew him in the way that men from the same general area and the same general tax bracket knew each other. He'd heard somewhere that Porter had got married awhile back. From the looks of the broad, he'd picked a real loser, but then, from the looks of them both, they probably deserved each other. Alderholt should have known better than to park his pregnant wife with a pair of booze hounds while he went table-hopping. Poor little mama was looking sicker by the minute.

Jake looked around at the large man in the plaid cummerbund, who had just risen and wandered over to another table, leaving his wife and his inebriated friends behind. Old Charlie must be at least sixty by now. Who'd have thought he'd wind up marrying again at his age, much less planting a brand new crop of little Alderholts.

Still staring absently at the Porter-Alderholt party, Jake turned his thoughts to his own family. He wondered what they were doing tonight. His wife had taken their five-year-old son and a baby-sitter to their beach place. Jake was to join them when and if he found time.

He should have gone with them. Johnny got tired on long trips. The baby-sitter was little more than a kid herself, and Cass wasn't noted for her patience in the best of circumstances. Civic duty be damned, he should never have allowed himself to be roped into this thing! Cass had bought the tickets and then changed her mind at the last minute, when it was too late for him to bow out. He should have just doubled the size of his annual check, mailed the damned thing in and gone to the beach to look after Johnny, but she'd insisted that one of them had to attend, and it had been easier to go along than to argue.

Of course, she was playing games again. He ought to be used to it by now, but he wasn't. Conquest was the name of the game, and he'd learned soon after they'd been married that while Cass thrived on the chase, she quickly grew bored with the catch. He'd hoped all that would change after Johnny was born, but evidently, it hadn't.

Jake's gaze strayed back to the pregnant blonde. Was she as miserable as she looked, or was she just laying a guilt trip on poor old Charlie because he wasn't dancing attention on her? Hell, she was here, wasn't she? Wearing a designer hatching jacket and about three carats of blue-white on her soft little hand?

Another bored socialite. Charlie should have known better than to marry a school kid and then ignore her. If there was one thing that drove Cass wild, it was to be ignored. By any male, regardless of age, financial bracket or marital status.

Jake belched discreetly. French cooking had never agreed with him. He shifted restlessly in his chair, waiting for the last speaker to run out of steam, for the band to start up, for people to start milling around so he could ease out the side door, his philanthropic duty done for another year.

He'd give a hundred bucks not to have eaten that damned yellow stuff with the blobs of black in the gravy! He'd give another hundred for a barbecue and beer.

Uh-oh. The blonde was in some kind of trouble, and Papa was nowhere in sight. Porter and his woman were too far gone to notice—either that or what she was doing to him under the table was about to render him *hors de combat.*

Jake snorted in disgust. It was no skin off his nose what they did, but little Mama looked as if she just might go into labor right here in the middle of the hotel ballroom.

His eyes narrowed as he watched for some sign. It was none of his business. God knows, he had enough trouble keeping his own marriage on track without borrowing from Charlie Alderholt, but somebody ought to do something.

Where the devil was Charlie, anyhow? Jake looked around, and then looked back at the blonde. Damned little fool had no business even being here. Charlie should've known better, even if she didn't.

Now she was leaning over toward Porter, tugging at his arm. Her eyes looked dark, almost panicky, in her pale face, and instinctively Jake began to ease his chair away from his table. He'd been seated with a couple he knew only slightly, both of whom had turned their chairs toward the front as soon as the speakers had begun.

Wake up, Porter, go haul your friend's ass back on-line and get him to take his wife home where she belongs!

But Porter, one arm around his own woman, only lifted the blonde's wrist from his sleeve as if it were something he'd found under a wet rock, and dropped it.

Stinking bastard, Jake thought dispassionately. Even if she wasn't his responsibility, no man had a right to treat any woman that way, especially one in her condition.

Jake stood and began making his way past the intervening tables with some notion of calling Porter's wife's attention to what was going on. Surely another woman wouldn't just brush her off that way. Just then a scattering of applause broke out and the restless audience began to break up.

A noisy party whom he vaguely remembered having met once or twice at the Gap moved between him and the Alderholt-Porter party. A woman with the figure of a ballpoint pen cried his name, flung her glittering fists on his chest and held up her cheek to be kissed, and by the time Jake got free again, little Mama was nearly at the door of the ballroom. "Mrs. Alderholt," he called, elbowing his way through the milling throng. She wasn't hard to follow. The crowd parted like the Red Sea as soon as they caught sight of her prominent condition.

"Mrs. Alderholt!" he called again, lunging to catch her arm just as she reached the heavy glass front doors. Where the hell was the doorman, anyway? Where the hell was her husband? Was the little fool deaf?

"Mrs. Alderholt, if you need—"

"Were you speaking to me?"

Her eyes reminded him of wet oak leaves. Dark, opaque green—red-rimmed now, with a smudge of mascara just beginning to puddle underneath. Blinking, she looked pointedly down at the hand on her arm, and Jake snatched it away.

"It's raining," he said, feeling like a fool now that he'd finally caught up with her.

"Yes." She lifted her chin as if the small defiant gesture alone could stop the rain, summon her pumpkin—and maybe turn poor old Charlie into Prince Charming.

"Mrs. Alderholt, I couldn't help but notice you were looking sort of...uncomfortable?" Damn, where was his brain? This was none of his business! Still, if she was going into labor, she didn't need to hang around all night waiting for Alderholt to tear himself away.

"I'm sorry, my name's not Alderholt," she said very quietly. "But thank you for your concern."

There was a brittleness about her that made Jake uneasy.

"Ma'am, if you'll wait right here—no, maybe you'd better sit down. Look, I'll go find Charlie and— Did you say you're not Mrs. Alderholt?"

"No, I'm not, but if you wouldn't mind finding me a taxi, I'd appreciate it very much," she said with a calmness he knew damned well was all wrong. There was a dignity about her that didn't jibe with red eyes, a bloated belly and swollen ankles, but Jake knew better than to argue with a woman. Especially a stranger. Especially a pregnant stranger!

He left to round up a cab. Collaring a doorman, he slipped him a folded bill and murmured, "Taxi. Make it five minutes ago, right?"

And then he was back again, hovering helplessly over the gravid female he had somehow got himself involved with. Fortunately the cab pulled up before he could blurt out a promise to go with her to whatever hospital she chose, stay with her during her ordeal and help her kid with his math homework if the need ever arose.

While his own car was brought around, Jake watched the taillights waver off down the wet street. He swore softly under his breath. What the hell was he doing, playing Don Quixote for some other man's woman? He had enough problems of his own!

One

_____

"Here she is, in all her glory, folks," Libby murmured softly to the woman in the mirror. Gray-streaked blond hair swept up for the occasion, a black silk designer dress, circa prepregnancy, black stockings with nary a runner in sight and a waistline that measured a full nine inches smaller than her 34 B cup. "Not bad," she whispered. "Not half-bad, all things considered."

So how come she kept seeing a plump frump in polyester and a ponytail, whose measurements didn't vary more than a couple of inches from one end of her torso to the other?

"Mama, can I have—"

"May I, David," Libby corrected automatically.

"May Billie and me have—"

Libby opened her mouth and closed it again.

"—some popcorn?"

"You and Billie may pop corn *after* supper, if Billie thinks you deserve a treat." There, that struck a balance, didn't it? No demands to clean off a plate, no threats concerning bedtime hour. She was learning, but it wasn't easy. Motherhood had never been easy, but at least now she didn't have someone else undermining her every effort at guidance. Now, if she could learn to be an effective father as well as an effective mother, David just might have a chance of growing up to be a well-adjusted individual, instead of a clone of the father he resembled so much.

Libby kissed her son goodbye, offered the baby-sitter, who also happened to be her cousin, a few last-minute suggestions and tried to ignore David's fleeting look of panic. It had taken five weeks before he would board the school bus without a scene. After that, she had started leaving him one or two evenings a month with Billie.

"I'm off, then. See you later, crocodile!"

"Mom, it's *alligator*," David said with a groan, and she slapped her forehead in mock chagrin.

The car started on the third try, which was encouraging. She checked the potholed driveway for balls, bats, bicycles and other natural hazards, and then she sniffed. Was her perfume too strong? Oh, heavens, she should have asked Billie.

The underwires of her black lace bra stabbed her in the armpit when she reached forward to release the emergency brake, and she wondered why in the world she hadn't worn something more comfortable. It wasn't as if anyone would know what color her underwear was, for pity sake!

Libby had no trouble finding the hotel after the twenty-five-minute drive into town. She'd scoped it out the week before when she'd taken David to the dentist. But at two in the afternoon, it hadn't looked quite so... big. The parking lot hadn't been quite so full, and there hadn't been all those glittery pink lights.

A long dark car glided to a halt before the canopied entrance, and a uniformed man stepped out to open the door. The parking attendant palmed a tip, slipped into the car and drove it off, and Libby watched the couple enter, wondering if they were there for the reunion. Wondering if she knew them.

Wondering if the heel of her ten-year-old black *peau de soie* pump was really loose, or if it only felt that way. Were pointed toes still in, or were they out again?

Blast. She should have worn her sneakers driving in, only she'd probably have forgotten and worn the things inside. Oh, blast!

Libby purely hated being intimidated. After enduring twelve years of being put down by an expert, not to mention by the most expensive divorce lawyer money could buy, she had sworn *never again!*

And here she was, cowering. Spineless as a raw egg! Afraid to go inside, afraid no one would know her—afraid they *would*—afraid she'd turn into an adolescent pumpkin again, and everyone would laugh.

She'd better get out of here. But then it would all be wasted. Oh, blast, why had she spent all that grocery money on a bottle of French toilet water?

Scowling, she sat there in her five-year-old station wagon, between the white Mercedes and the big black Ford, and ran through the routine once more. "Listen, wimp, they're not even going to remember you!"

You hope.

"And even if they do, do you think they're all just dying to discover how fat-face Libby Dwiggins happened to wind up with a waistline, a designer dress and an over-dose of *eau de toilette?* Ha!''

Tired of arguing with herself, Libby braced her shoulders and tilted her chin. She took a deep breath and reached for the door handle, then changed her mind and switched on the local news station, telling herself she might as well catch the weather report before she went inside. Living in the country, it paid to keep abreast of things like that.

Sighing, she had just begun to nibble off her lipstick when someone leaned down to breathe whiskey fumes in through her half-open window. ''Well, hel-*lo* there, li'l darlin'. You been waitin' out here all by your lonesome? Ol' Pete would never keep a lady waitin'. Why'n'cha move over, hmmm?''

Libby hastily began to roll up the window, but the drunk shoved his elbow in where his fingers had been before. ''C'mon, now, honey, don' be like that. Ol' Pete jus' wants to show you a good time. Ol' Pete likes li'l—''

Suddenly old Pete was lying flat on his back on the pavement, and a large man in a dark suit was dusting off his hands.

Libby gaped through the partially open window. She was still gaping when the stranger dragged the drunk across the parking lot, draped him decorously across one of the black marble planters that flanked the front entrance, and sauntered back to her station wagon.

Finally she gathered her wits enough to squeak out her thanks.

''Don't mention it,'' the man said dryly.

Jake had been sitting in his own car when the blonde had pulled in beside him. He'd given her an automatic once-over, his mind on other matters, and then done a slow double take. Did he know her? Was she someone he ought to remember? If so, he was going to be embarrassed when he couldn't come up with her name.

Ah, hell, this had been a lousy idea from the beginning. He'd trashed the letter of invitation as soon as he'd got it, but then, after thinking about it all day, he'd gone back, unlocked his office and retrieved the damned thing before the cleaning crew came by. He seemed to recall entertaining some pseudo-philosophic notion that if he couldn't face the past, he didn't stand a snowball's chance of building any kind of a future.

Which was sheer bilge. He'd already *built* his future. At least, he was a damn sight closer to it than he would ever have believed possible a few years ago.

His gaze strayed back to the blonde. *Did* he know her? The hotel was full of people, not all here for the same reason, but she was about the right age. Jake was forty. She looked a few years younger, but then, he was older than the rest of his graduating class, thanks to a fool stunt that had gotten his neck broken and cost him a couple of years.

With more interest than he'd shown any woman in a long time, John Hatcher Healy, alias Jake Hatcher, leaned against his car and studied the woman in the pink neon glow. She ought to know by now that her kind of hair was too heavy to wear in that style. It was the slick, straight kind of hair that always lost out to the law of gravity. Nice style while it lasted, though. Her neck was long, slender, unusually elegant. Jake had never been a neck man, but he had enough of a classical education to recognize the beauty of hers.

Did he know her? Probably not. He would have remembered.

He saw her lift that well-defined jaw another degree, as
if she were aware of his scrutiny. Somewhere in the back
of his mind, a bell began to clang softly.

Yeah, there was something familiar about that attitude, all right. He might not remember her name or her
face—it had been twenty years, after all, and a lot had
happened in the meantime. A lot that he had sworn to put
behind him.

But he remembered that chin. He'd been wondering
about it when he'd seen the drunk stagger up to her car
and try to put the moves on her. He'd lay odds it wasn't
the first time she'd reacted to danger by leading with her
chin. As a big-time loser doing his damnedest to make a
comeback, Jake could have told her she was just asking
for trouble.

The hotel doors opened and a small group spilled out,
accompanied by the sounds of revelry from the ballroom
across the lobby. The party was getting ripe. *Okay,
Hatcher, decision time. You gonna go inside? Or you
gonna hang around the parking lot all night?*

Jake levered his rangy, six-two frame away from his car,
turned toward the entrance and then suddenly swung back
toward the blonde in the station wagon. Leaning down to
her window, he rasped, "Look, lady, I don't know what
your problem is, but if you're going to sit out here in the
dark looking for trouble, you just might find more than
you bargained for."

"No, I—that is, I'm going inside. The reunion. That is,
I'm..."

"Chicken," Jake said softly, and watched, amused, as
she cranked that elegant little chin up another degree or
two. It might work on some men. It hadn't on the drunk.
It wouldn't on a man like Jake, either, he told himself.
Which was why he couldn't figure what the devil he was

doing, wrenching her door open a moment later to slide onto the passenger seat beside her.

"What are you— Get out of my car!"

"Lady, you've got the brains of a bedbug. What the hell do you mean, sitting out here in an unlocked car? Didn't your mama teach you anything?" Her mouth was hanging open, and he wondered why her parents had never bothered to put her in braces when she was a kid. Although the slight overlap probably added a certain distinction to her smile. If she ever smiled.

"I told you I'm going inside!"

"Sure you are," he drawled. "That's why you've been sitting here for the past twenty minutes, right? Trying to figure out which foot to put first."

"Do you make a habit of accosting strange women in parking lots?"

"Hell, honey, you're not all *that* strange. A little slow, maybe, but—"

Blindly Libby reached for her purse, which had fallen behind the console. With one hand on the door handle, she was ready to jump and run when his next words made her pause.

"I'm sorry. I don't usually butt in this way, but—"

"Oh, I expect you do. You're too good at it to be an amateur."

In spite of his irritation, Jake chuckled. "Yeah, maybe you're right."

"And I ought to thank you. I do thank you. For earlier. The drunk, I mean. I probably shouldn't have left the window open, but—" But her car smelled like wet sneakers, thanks to David.

"You shouldn't have left the window open or the door unlocked. In fact, you shouldn't be here at all."

"I reached the same conclusion not ten minutes ago. About being here, I mean. People shouldn't try to turn back the clock. It never works."

"The reunion?"

"Uh-huh. It's my class, but..." From the corners of her eyes, Libby studied the stranger, who was lounging against the far door. He hadn't made a single threatening move, other than being there. On the other hand, if he hadn't been there a few minutes ago, she would have had to deal with the drunk herself. And while she didn't doubt that she could have handled it—she could have opened the door suddenly and knocked him down, then locked her doors and leaned on the horn—still, she hadn't, and he had, and she owed him for that.

"Yeah, me, too," the man said, and she turned to study him more openly.

"Do I know you?" Black hair, with more than a touch a gray. Eyes dark—maybe brown, maybe not. Mouth...

The term *bitter* came to mind, and she wondered briefly at the description and then went on with her mental inventory. He looked as if he'd come up the hard way, but at least he had made it, if that suit he was wearing was anything to go by.

Libby knew about men's clothing. Walt, her ex-husband, had spent more on his own back in a month than she and David together spent in a year. For a man whose family had been rolling in money for generations, Walt was surprisingly miserly where his wife and son were concerned. But then, that was just one more of his little cruelties. Making her beg for every penny and then criticizing her for the way she dressed.

"Figured it out yet?"

Startled, Libby shook her head, and then reached up to shove in the pins that slipped from her upswept hair.

"Sorry. It's been a long time and my eyes aren't what they used to be." Which was why she was wearing her contacts.

"Right. You'll probably hear that excuse more than once tonight, that is if you're planning on going inside."

"Are you?" Libby asked tentatively. Maybe it wouldn't be so scary if she had someone to hide behind the first few minutes.

"Are you?" he countered.

"What's the matter, don't tell me you're afraid to go in there."

"As you said, it's been a long time, and I doubt that I'll remember many faces. I haven't kept up with anyone from the past."

"Then why'd you come?"

Jake shrugged. He'd asked himself that same question more than once since he'd left home tonight. He still didn't know. Some kind of symbolism, he supposed, but damned if he intended to try to explain that to some middle-aged housewife dressed up in her Sunday best. "Look, if you want to, we could go in together, look the old gang over, pay our respects and then get the hell out, duty done for the next twenty years." The offer surprised Jake as much as it surprised the woman.

"I'm game if you are," Libby replied. "To tell the truth, I hate like the devil to have gone to all this trouble and expense for nothing."

The tickets hadn't been that much. Just enough to cover the costs, Jake figured. As if reading his mind, she said, "Not just the ticket, but my new scent. I think I overdid it."

Leaning over, he dutifully sniffed the air near her right cheek. "Just right. Je Reviens?" he asked, and even in the semidarkness, he could see her eyes widen. They were large, possibly green, and either her lashes were naturally dark or she had a deft hand with mascara. For some reason, he was pretty sure it was nature's quirky gift. Pale blond hair, much too glossy to have come from a bottle, and dark brows and lashes. Cassie would've killed for a combination like that.

"You're good," Libby said admiringly as she let herself out. Either that or he'd known a lot of women.

Jake met her halfway around the car. "Jake Hatcher," he said. "I figure if we start out knowing even one other person at this bash, we'll be ahead of the game."

Libby grinned, and Jake decided he'd been right about the tooth. It definitely added something. "Libby Porter," she said. "I used to be Libby Dwiggins."

He'd been right about that, too. The name didn't ring any bells. "Nice to know you, Libby Porter. Shall we?" He extended an elbow, and she tucked her hand in the crook.

The band was loud, but surprisingly good. Libby winced, and Jake leaned down and murmured against her ear, "Maybe they supply earplugs. I could ask." Evidently she wasn't a regular patron of nightclubs. The decibel level was about average.

"I'm pretty good at reading lips. I'll manage."

"Bombs away, then. Uh-oh. Name tags at two o'clock. Want to take evasive action?"

"If that's who I think it is, evasive action isn't going to do us any good. Hall monitor, secretary of everything, worst snitch in school."

"I thought she looked familiar. She collared me once for posting a vacancy sign on old Harry's hat." Old Harry being the principal. Jake smiled at the approaching woman and reached out to scoop up two tags from among the few left, ignoring her look of avid curiosity.

"We'll take these, thanks," he told her, and turning away, he frowned down at Libby's V-necked dress with the modest shoulder pads and narrow belted waist. "Uh ... where shall I put it?"

"How about that waste can over there behind the bar?"

"Right." Jake disposed of the tags and after a brief conference with the bartender, returned with two drinks. "White wine all right?" His own was seltzer in a wineglass. With an olive. It had been a long, dry spell, but some lessons a man didn't have to learn twice.

After half an hour of mingling, peering at name tags and explaining that their own had gotten mixed up and were in the process of being replaced, Jake steered Libby toward a bank of potted jungle. "Look, I don't want to cramp your style, Libby. If you want to wing it, feel free. Now that I've got my bearings, I'll be okay."

Libby tried not to let her disappointment show. It was hardly the first brush-off she'd experienced, and this one at least had the advantage of being polite.

"Sure. I'm okay now, too," she said, smiling as if she weren't tempted to dive under the nearest palm tree. "And Jake, thanks for everything. Out there, I mean—and this." She waved a hand vaguely toward the gyrating couples on the dance floor.

"Look, if you want to dance or anything—" he began, but she shook her head quickly.

"Oh, no! That is, thanks, but no thanks. I don't."

"Don't, or won't?"

"Can't. Don't know how. Not very well, at least."

Shrugging, Jake reached up and captured one of her hairpins just before it fell, shoved it in and then stepped back. "That I can't believe," he countered gently.

"Believe it. I was born with two left feet."

Jake glanced down at her trim feet in the fragile silk shoes. He said nothing, simply lifting his thick black brows.

"But look, don't let me stop you. See that woman over there in the green sequins, with the long red hair? She's a terrific dancer. I've been watching her. I think her name's Candy or something or other. Why not go over and renew an old friendship?"

Jake followed her gaze, sized up the woman in question and shrugged again. If she wanted to get rid of him, no problem. He hadn't planned on adopting her. "I can't quite place her."

"Don't worry, I expect she'll place you," Libby said softly. Jake shrugged, and a moment later she was watching him weave his way across the crowded floor. She didn't know Jake Hatcher from Adam's off ox, but one thing she was sure of. He wasn't the sort of man any woman could forget, not if she'd ever experienced that sexy, masculine appeal of his at close range. Libby had known arrogant men before. Walt, for instance. But unlike her ex-husband, Jake's arrogance had nothing to do with what he owned and everything to do with who he was.

As she watched the green-sequined redhead react to Jake like kudzu on a pine tree, Libby reminded herself that she had room in her life for only one male, and that male was her son, David. This whole reunion thing had been a mistake. It wasn't as if she had any real friends from her high school days. She'd been the quintessential nerdess, the butt of everyone's favorite jokes.

"I thought I recognized that blond mop of yours. Libby Dwiggins?"

Libby spun around at the sound of a friendly voice. Her gaze went up and up and up, and her eyes widened. "Kenny? Kenny Smith?"

"Hey, you remembered me!"

"As if I could ever forget the only member of the senior class who was nice to me when being nice to Libby Dwiggins wasn't cool! Oh, Kenny, how in the world *are* you?"

He hugged her and held her away, silently pursing his lips as his gaze roved over her with brief, if flattering, attention. "Hey, look at you! I knew I should've put in my bid before the rush started." He reached for her left hand and touched the ring on her third finger. It was an inexpensive one she'd bought herself—her freedom ring, she called it. She had put away Walt's gaudy diamond set for David, but she hadn't felt quite right without something on the third finger of her left hand.

They talked about Kenny's job as a social worker in New Jersey, and Libby told him about moving back into her old home, and they laughed and tried to pick out familiar faces. The sweet-faced butterball in pink was the head cheerleader. Oh, and wasn't that the star quarterback? The one with the beer belly? He still wore the sideburns that had been popular back then, and Libby felt a sudden, quite unexpected kinship with him.

"That's Ted Smith, the football star, isn't it?"

"Yeah—I think he owns his own garage now."

"I used to have the most awful crush on him," she confessed.

"Mine was on Cheryl." The cheerleader. "Remember that last game, when I tripped and spilled a hot dog loaded with chili in her lap?"

Libby laughed, and Kenny led her out onto the floor before she quite realized what he was doing. Having reached the lofty altitude of six feet eight in junior high school, he'd been something of a misfit, too, although basketball had saved him from complete social ostracism.

But he'd always been kind, and as Libby bumped knees and toes in an attempt to follow his lead, she told herself she might have known he would end up helping others the same way he had helped her through a miserable adolescence.

Jake, leaning against the wall, sipped at his third seltzer and watched the two laughing people galloping gracelessly across the floor. She'd been right. She wasn't very good. But then, with that tall drink of water for a partner, it was small wonder.

She really came alive when she laughed. Her hair was nearly undone by now, the shaggy coil brushing her shoulders. Her cheeks were flushed and her eyes—they were green, just as he'd thought—sparkled like wet oak leaves. Good or not, she wouldn't have any trouble finding partners.

Handing his glass to a passing waiter, Jake left. Coming here had been a waste of time. He'd run into several guys he used to know, but then, when he'd introduced himself as Jake Hatcher, they'd looked puzzled. Not wanting to get into explanations of why he'd dropped his last name when he'd started the long climb out of the gutter, he'd moved on.

Of course, the redhead was another matter. Candy Travers. Twice divorced, and game to try her luck again. She'd remembered him, remembered his name, and made it pretty obvious that she was more than willing to pick up where they'd left off before. Which, if he remembered correctly, had been at a house party in Blowing Rock, in an indoor Olympic-size pool . . . sans suits.

Two

With Billie asleep in the guest room and David, his mouth showing vestiges of a toothpaste mustache, sleeping soundly in his bunk bed, Libby hung up her black dress, changed into her pajamas and dragged out one of several boxes she had yet to unpack since moving back home after her divorce.

Oops! Maternity clothes. She *definitely* wouldn't be needing those again. Oh, and here was her great-grandmother's blue bowl. It was one of the few things from her family that Walt had coveted, and she'd delighted in reminding him that under the terms of their agreement, it was not marital property. After so much humiliation, she had savored the small triumph.

Another box held her old stamp collection, an unused photograph album and a bundle of twenty-year-old letters from a pen pal in Holland. Ancient history.

Naturally it was in the last box she searched in. Libby remembered telling someone who had made the same remark once that it would be silly to go on looking after finding what they were searching for in the first place they looked. For her troubles she had earned a dirty look and a snide remark.

Dusting her hand on the seat of her pajamas, she pulled out the high school annual and leaned her back against the washing machine as she began leafing through it. There were hardly any autographs. No one had offered and she hadn't had the nerve to ask. Except for Kenny Smith, who had scrawled some illegible sentiment, wishing her either gut cheese and jag, or good cheer and joy.

Funny how pinched all the faces looked. And how very young. Dwiggins, Libby. No clubs, no superlatives. Her grades had made her eligible for Honor Society, but she'd never been invited to join, and she'd lacked the courage to ask. Poor, pudgy little dumpling, her earnest, nearsighted glare hidden behind owlish plastic-rimmed glasses. No wonder she hadn't attracted many friends!

Libby flipped the pages. It wasn't her own picture she'd been searching for. F, G, H . . . Hall, Haltzer, Hawthorn. No Hatcher. She closed the book and dropped it back inside the carton, along with her old college textbooks and several *Man From U.N.C.L.E.* comic books.

Dammit, she *did* remember him! He looked different after twenty years, but she was almost certain she remembered him . . . only the name Hatcher wasn't in the book, and neither was his picture.

The rest of the week passed uneventfully, and by the middle of the following week Libby had all but forgotten Jake Hatcher and the class reunion. She called Aunt Lula over in Davie County to tell her how much she appreciated being able to count on Billie to baby-sit occasionally, and listened to a compendium of advice in the event she should ever find herself stricken with lower-back pain.

After seeing David off on the school bus, Libby started the wash, smeared on a film of lip gloss and grabbed her purse. She had a dozen errands to do, including depositing Walt's child-support check, which had been late, as usual. She suspected he deliberately delayed it, hoping she would call and beg. One of his favorite games had been keeping her short of money so she would have to ask for whatever she needed. It gave him a sense of power.

According to one of their mutual friends, Sara Dwyer, Walt had always been a control freak, even in kindergarten. Sara had grown up with Walt, attending the same exclusive schools, their families summering at the same exclusive resorts. Surprisingly Sara and Libby had become good friends, but when the split came, Sara had sided with Walt. Like to like. It wasn't enough that Walt got to keep the house they had built together, the cottage at Roaring Gap and the two newest cars—the wretch even got to keep their friends!

But in the end, Libby kept the only thing she truly valued. For months, ever since it became obvious that her marriage was disintegrating, the question of custody had terrified her. Walt's family owned half the county, including the best law firm within three hundred miles. By the time the divorce papers were signed, she had lost all the weight she'd gained back after David was born, and all of the self-confidence, too.

Walt had used the threat of taking David from her to cut even the minimal settlement allowed her in the prenuptial agreement, and she had been too frightened to realise that it was an empty threat. Besides, Walt didn't really want a child underfoot. He had told her more than once that he'd played the husband-father bit long enough to know that it really wasn't his thing. At forty he was eager to cut his losses and try something new.

By that time, Libby had been only too glad to be cut, but David was another matter. The first time she had come upon her son crying and asking why Daddy didn't like him anymore, the dregs of a long-dead love had been flushed away for good. If it wasn't for David, Libby would have taken great pleasure in throwing his tiny settlement back in his face, but pride wouldn't put food on the table or a roof over David's head, and with David needing her more than ever, she couldn't very well go out and find a job that would support them both, even if jobs were plentiful for middle-aged, inexperienced women. The prenuptial agreement hadn't left much room for negotiation, but at least she'd been able to get a reasonable amount of child support.

Ten years earlier, in the throes of her first and only love affair, Libby would have signed away her right arm if Walt had asked her to. He'd been handsome, charming and extremely wealthy, although she hadn't known it at the time. When she had finally realized just which family of Porters he belonged to, and what they stood for in that area, she couldn't believe he had wanted her.

Of course by that time, she had lost her puppy fat, and as the uniform of the day had been blue jeans, she had been right in style. Country was in, and Libby was nothing if not country. The genuine article, as her New York City roommate had proclaimed.

Then, too, she had still been a virgin. That had evidently been something of a novelty in Walt's circle of friends.

When the time came, she had signed the agreement. She would have signed her own death warrant if he'd asked her to, but he had assured her that it was only a formality. "See, the thing is, my family owns this law firm, and they think they have to do these things to earn their keep. It doesn't mean a thing, sweetheart, it's just a formality."

And blindly, blithely in love, she had signed away her rights. The next time she had given it a thought it had been when Walt had told her that in light of that same agreement, she should consider herself damned lucky. As it was, he was being more than generous in the amount of child support he was willing to pay.

"Generous, my sweet fanny," Libby muttered now as she whipped into the bank's parking lot. At least she'd had sense enough to get away from Raleigh. Her parents had moved to Florida, and her old home had been between tenants, most of the farmland having long since been sold off to finance her parents' retirement. The house was old, but it was comfortably familiar, with plenty of room for a large garden and maybe even a few chickens. Libby had rented it from her parents, who hadn't wanted to take her money, but she'd told them that Walt insisted.

Ha!

Naturally there was a line at the bank. Lunch-hour traffic. Libby fidgeted. She wanted to get back in time to hang the clothes out, because if she used the dryer, the little dials on the electric service meter spun around like a souped-up top.

"Libby?"

This time it was Libby who spun around, her heart slamming up against her faded Zoological Society T-shirt. "Jake! What are you doing here?"

"Nothing illegal, I assure you." Grinning, Jake thought this was more like it. T-shirt and jeans, sneakers and ponytail. A touch of gray, but it blended with the gold into a damned attractive amalgam. He hadn't planned on following up their first meeting, but on the other hand, he'd never been one to sneer at fate. "How about you?"

"Last in a long list of errands. The monthly deposit."

Alimony, probably. He'd wondered if she was divorced when he'd noticed the ring on her third finger, left hand. It wasn't a wedding band, but as it was the only ring she wore, he figured it must have some significance. Besides, her name hadn't been Porter back in high school.

"Have you had lunch?" he asked.

"I seldom bother." Libby's mind shifted automatically into a defensive position. He was going to invite her to lunch. She would have to insist on paying her own way, and she couldn't afford it, having blown far too much on that blasted reunion thing.

"Seldom bother to *eat?*"

Taking her place before a free teller, Libby handed over her deposit, already made out, and turned back to Jake. "To eat lunch. I always eat a good breakfast and a good dinner, so that—but why am I telling you this?"

Jake's eyes twinkled. Under the bank's bright lights, he looked even more attractive than she'd remembered. There were deep grooves bracketing the mouth she had first thought of as bitter—and saw no reason now to change her mind. He had the kind of cheekbones that made his skin stretch leather-tight down over a solid jaw. Altogether a formidable face, she decided—except for the eyes. Why was it that underneath the twinkle, she sensed so much sadness? So much pain? She sensed it, wondered at it briefly and then mentally began to back away.

"Look, I'd better dash," she told him with a blinding, lap-toothed smile. "I still have to—but it was nice seeing you again, and—oh, goodness, would you look at the time!''

With the delicate precision of a forty-ton bulldozer, Jake plowed through her polite excuses. ''You don't eat lunch, but you do eat dinner, right?''

Libby snatched at her deposit slip and took a step backward. Moving up to the counter, Jake slid over a thick envelope without ever releasing her from those dark, compelling eyes. ''Okay, so we'll have dinner.''

Panic struck, and she began to back out the exit lane. ''Oh, no, I couldn't. I have to—that is, I promised—''

''No problem. We don't have to make it tonight. I've got a meeting tomorrow night, but how about Thursday? About seven?''

''Jake, I—''

''What are you afraid of?''

''Afraid?'' Libby nibbled at her lower lip. Was she afraid?

Damned right she was afraid! And it wasn't just because of the way that David might react. Since the separation he had reacted with either embarrassing hostility or equally embarrassing adulation to every adult male she had spoken with even casually. After years of Walt's neglect, he was so starved for masculine attention that she hadn't dared think about dating, even if she'd had the opportunity.

''What's your address?''

''I don't have an address. That is, I do, but it's a rural route number.'' Why am I even considering this? she asked herself frantically. This man has danger written all over him! Caution: Jake Hatcher may be hazardous to your heart!

''Okay then, tell me how to find you. Oh, and what kind of food do you like? Ethnic? Steak? Seafood?''

Libby dropped her deposit slip, bent over to pick it up and collided with Jake halfway down. He kissed his fingertip, placed it on her forehead the way she'd done to David a hundred times, and her defenses crumbled like a paper fortress. "Tell you what, we'll wait and decide which restaurant later. Now, how about those directions?"

It might have been sunspot activity. It might be the holes in the ozone layer. Whatever the cause, Libby's mature, well-insulated brain suddenly shorted out. Fizzle, sizzle, zap! She heard herself saying, "Look, why don't I just meet you somewhere? There's this Mexican place—"

"Casa Gallardo, Tijuana Fats, Casa Azul, Casa—"

"That one. Azul whatever." She'd heard Billie mention it last week as having good, affordable food.

"You're the boss," he conceded. "So it's Thursday night, seven, in the lobby. I'll see you there."

Libby drove home in a daze. What on earth had come over her? She had neither the time nor the emotional energy to waste on getting involved with a man, and she was very much afraid that any dealings at all with a man like Jake Hatcher would constitute involvement. On her part, at least.

It was that sneaky shot about her being the boss. If the man had deliberately aimed for her biggest weakness, he couldn't have scored higher!

On Thursday night Libby changed her dress four times and finally settled for her gray-black-and-gold paisley slacks with the dark gray knit top. Walt had hated the outfit from the moment she'd told him that she'd bought it on sale at a discount store.

Billie had been recruited once more, and Libby explained to David that she was only going out to dinner with an old school mate.

"Can I imbite Jeff to dinner at our house?"

"May I, David. And of course you may in*vite* Jeff," Libby said as she hugged her son good-night. It was the first time he had asked to have any of his new friends over. She took it as a good sign.

Libby had never been comfortable in social situations, although for a while after her marriage to a wealthy, extremely social Raleigh man, she had learned to play the part with some success. Once her marriage had started coming apart, however, she had concentrated all her energies on being there for David. Since moving back to her home town, she had gone alone to a few movies, a few lectures and one high school reunion, using them as an excuse to ask her cousin Billie to come baby-sit.

She had done it far more for David's sake than for her own, needing to prove to him that even though she left him for a few hours, he could trust her to return. Each time, he seemed a little more secure, but Libby knew he was still struggling with his anger for what his parents had done to him. At this stage, his moods seemed to swing between fierce dependence and equally fierce independence.

Casa Azul was easy enough to find, and Libby pulled in only three cars away from where Jake sat waiting. He was there to help her out almost before she had set the parking brake. She looked up, blinked and took a deep breath, bracing herself to accept the hand he held out to her.

Oh, mercy. Did all men look so incredibly sexy under night lighting? Was it the setting, or was it just Jake?

Or was she getting weird in her old age?

"What are you sighing about?" he murmured, the sound of his voice as deep and raspy as a lion's purr.

"You wouldn't believe me if I told you."

"Try me."

She thought quickly and came up with the most plausible excuse she could think of. "That wasn't a sigh, it was my stomach growling. I'm starving," she said, and Jake threw back his head and laughed.

"Yeah. Me, too," he said, still chuckling as he ushered her inside. It occurred to Jake that he had laughed more in the short time he had known her than in all the past seven years.

He offered her wine, but because she had to drive home later, Libby declined. So did Jake. She considered it a mark in his favor. Walt had never let a little thing like driving afterward keep him from enjoying a party to the fullest. Which meant that Libby had never been able to enjoy them at all, for he wouldn't hear of her driving his high-priced European sports car.

It had been one more reason for her to stop going to parties, not that Walt had protested her staying home. He'd already made it painfully obvious that he would never lack female companionship.

Stop thinking like a wife and begin thinking like a woman, Libby reminded herself. But not *too* much like a woman, she amended cautiously.

As if by mutual consent, they stuck to safe topics, such as politics and religion. Libby didn't ask what Jake did for a living, or what he'd been doing these past twenty years. In return, Jake respected Libby's privacy enough not to ask about the ring on her finger, about the shadows behind those sudden, almost-too-bright smiles, or the calluses on her small, beautifully shaped hands. They were both careful to avoid touching on the personal, yet by the end of the evening, each felt they knew the other considerably better than before.

Jake found himself enjoying her quirky sense of humor and her independence. As a general rule he found fiercely independent women a bit abrasive for his taste, but there was a gentleness about Libby Porter, a vulnerability even, that struck a responsive chord deep inside him, and he admitted to himself that with any encouragement at all he might find himself sexually attracted to her. Still, as that encouragement didn't seem forthcoming, he saw no reason why they couldn't enjoy the occasional evening out. Convivial, congenial companionship. Nothing threatening on either side.

Libby was relaxed. She was also tired. She had breezed through her usual chores to leave herself time to clean the gutters, put up a new clothesline and repair a broken back step. Now she stifled a yawn. They were on their fourth cup of after-dinner coffee, having both declined dessert, when Jake said casually, "The band at the hotel the other night wasn't half-bad. I understand they play there every weekend, if you'd like to try your luck at dancing."

She grinned and shook her head. "Thanks anyway. I doubt if your insurance covers the hazard of dancing with Libby Porter."

"Ever hear of steel-toed shoes?" He stood and held her chair, and Libby glanced down at his size twelves. Jake was a large man, in all respects.

"I've never heard of steel-toed dancing slippers."

"Didn't you ever take ballet lessons?"

"You saw me with Kenny Smith at the reunion. Did it look to you as if I'd studied ballet?" She laughed, and Jake decided braces just might be overrated. There was something to be said for a less-than-perfect smile. A lot to be said for hers, in fact.

* * *

A week later Jake called and asked Libby to go dancing with him at the hotel where they had first met. Hearing her start to refuse and then hesitate, he wondered if maybe, like him, she occasionally got tired of staring at one more in a long line of empty evenings alone.

"Of course, if you've got other plans," he said. Hell, what made him think he was the only man she knew?

"Jake, I told you I'm not much of a dancer."

"We don't have to dance if you don't want to. We can listen to the music, watch other couples, have dinner and unwind. I need it, even if you don't, and if I don't go out, I'll just end up working."

"Oh, so you're one of those, hmm?"

"Afraid so."

"All right, but I'm warning you, if you insist on dancing, don't say I didn't warn you."

"I think you've managed to get your point across." He grinned. Wondering if she was smiling, too, he found himself picturing that lap-toothed grin of hers and smiling even more broadly.

At thirty-eight, Libby's skin was considerably thicker than it had been back in her more impressionable years. The fact that no boy had ever asked her to dance until she was too old to learn gracefully was pretty low on her list of things to worry herself sleepless over. All the same, she wished she had taken advantage of a few lessons back when she could have afforded it. Walt wasn't a dancer, either—at least not with his own wife.

The days dragged by, but finally the weekend rolled around. Jake was picking her up at home, and she debated inviting him in to meet David, but for David's sake, she decided against it. If he got his hopes up over the man who had come to pump out the septic tank, a man who spit and swore and had a naked woman tattooed on his right bicep, she didn't dare take the risk of exposing him to Jake Hatcher.

With a cheerful wave and a final word of advice to Billie, Libby let herself out as soon as she heard the crunch of tires on her graveled driveway. Jake was already halfway up the front walk. She met him there, and without comment other than to say that she was prompt, he took her arm and reversed directions.

They didn't talk much on the way into town. Libby toyed with the handle of her purse and cut frequent glances toward Jake's profile. It would have looked right at home on Mount Rushmore, she decided. Forcing her eyes deliberately to the front, she inhaled the subtle scent of leather upholstery and a masculine cologne—cedar, sandalwood, citrus?

Oh, Lord, something tells me this was a big mistake.

The doorman was suitably obsequious, the food excellent for all it tasted like wet cardboard to Libby, and the music didn't seem quite so loud as she remembered. Certainly no woman could have asked for a more attractive, more attentive dinner date. She told herself that maybe her luck was finally turning. She might not be any man's dream lover, but she was here, wasn't she? Jake was looking at her as if she were more interesting than the wallpaper, which was a novelty in itself. Walt had spent so much time staring over the top of her head whenever they went out to eat that she'd often been tempted to feel for a halo... or horns.

And if she needed any other evidence that where there was life there was hope, David had brought home a friend from school and they had played quietly for more than two hours without a fight. And the foot valve on the well pump had only been waterlogged, so she wasn't going to have to buy a new pump. And the weather had turned cool enough so that she could wear her favorite dress, one she'd splurged on back in the days before she'd lost her last illusion of a happy ever after.

"Penny for them," Jake murmured.

"Weather, illusions, fights and foot valves."

His eyes widened. They were dark, neither brown nor gray, but an oddly attractive blend of both. "What are you, a meteorologist, a magician or an engineer?"

She laughed. "You left out the fights. Actually, none of the above. Harried home owner. Mine's not exactly new, in case you didn't notice."

"You live with your parents?" He'd wondered about that. It wasn't too surprising that a woman, either divorced or temporarily unemployed, might move back home to care for aging parents.

"My parents retired to a one-bedroom house in a one-streetlight town in Florida. They think it's heaven. I still have family in the area, of course. Aunts, uncles, cousins..."

And a son. One very dear, very troubled, very wonderful son. "And a—" she started to say.

But Jake apparently didn't want to talk about family, hers or his. For an instant, his face tensed, all expression wiped away. It happened so quickly that Libby thought she must have imagined it, especially when he stood and reached for her hand. "Steel toes," he said with that lazy, familiar grin. "Shin guards, too, just in case you're a high stepper. So do your worst, lady, I'm ready for you."

With a demureness that would have shocked her had she even been aware of it, Libby accepted his hand, stood and moved into his arms. "How can I refuse such a gracious invitation?"

Later she would blame it on the slow, seductive melody, an old love song from the forties she vaguely remembered hearing her mother sing while working in the kitchen. On the other hand, Jake's cologne, as subtle as it was, was not entirely innocent of blame.

The last thing on earth she wanted to blame was those arms that held her as if she were infinitely fragile, infinitely precious, and the hard chest that somehow drew her cheek to rest against it as they slowly swayed to the music.

Jake didn't actually dance. What he did do was hold her so that every square inch of her body was electrically alive, inside and out, to every square inch of his. Libby forgot to breathe, and when she remembered, she had to concentrate on the process so intently that she forgot she couldn't dance.

"See?" Jake murmured against her ear. He had to lower his head, because even with her three-inch heels, her ear barely came up to his shoulder. "I told you you could dance."

"Is that what we're doing?" she blurted out before she could control her tongue. "I didn't say what you just heard. I didn't say a thing."

He chuckled. Resting his cheek against the top of her head, he swayed gently from side to side, and after a while it occurred to Libby that neither of them had moved their feet in some time.

"Smart man. You knew I wouldn't be such a hazard as long as I didn't move my feet while we were dancing."

His arms tightened until she could feel his rib cage, feel the shape of his masculine hips. "Honey, that's where you're dead wrong. As hazards go, I'd rank you right up there with live volcanoes and acid rain."

As soon as she regained control of her tongue, Libby reminded him that it was getting late. Jake didn't argue. They were silent on the way home, and this time Libby knew better than to look at him. Halfway out of town, Jake switched on a classical music station, which reduced some of the tension that had sprung up between them.

Merciful heavens, what had she been thinking of? Had she honestly thought she was immune? Just because she had never slept with any man but Walt, and that had ended years ago, did she think her sexual nature had been permanently laid to rest?

Maybe it had. These days the one-man, one-woman system was about the only safe course, and even that was not without hazards. Besides, she wasn't anywhere near ready to even think about ... that sort of thing.

"Look, um ... I'm going to be out of town for a couple of weeks," Jake said as they neared her turnoff.

"Yes, well, I've just remembered that I promised to visit my aunt and uncle, and I can't put it off much longer." She twisted her purse handle again. The gold-chain handle hadn't been designed for such service. It broke, and she retrieved her purse from the floor.

"So I guess we'll both be tied up for a while," Jake said, and numbly, Libby nodded.

Nothing had changed, she told herself as she let herself inside after a brusque and rather hurried good-night. Nothing at all. She was following the same familiar pattern. Like a hungry, homeless mutt, falling all over her own clumsy feet to lavish affection on someone who neither needed it nor wanted it.

Three

———

Jake sprawled in the oversize leather chair and stared at the bottle of Scotch whiskey, feeling only the faintest wisp of regret. It had been years since he had given in to the temptation. Of alcohol, at least.

One demon at a time, Jake, old man—one demon at a time.

Weaknesses of the flesh came in a multitude of forms. The one he was currently wrestling didn't happen to come in a bottle. Instead it had slipped past his guard in the guise of a stubborn-jawed female with a glossy crop of gray-blond hair, eyes the color of oak leaves and hips that flared sweetly from a waist he could almost span with his two hands.

Libby Porter. Libby—what had she said she'd been before? Wiggins? Priggins?

Whatever. She'd been married at least once. Which meant that she was now widowed or divorced or separated. Regardless of all he *didn't* know about her, Jake was pretty sure she wasn't the type to run around on a current husband. Some women, maybe. Some women surely! But not Libby Porter.

So... did he want her enough to risk getting involved, or didn't he?

For the first year or so after Johnny—after Cassie—Jake had been in freefall. It had been in a one-cell jail in a one-horse town in southwest Virginia, where he'd woken up with two black eyes, a broken nose and a right hand the size of a Smithfield ham, that he had finally been forced to face up to what he'd become.

Moose Capehart had been a year behind him in high school. The kid had been shooting for a football scholarship until he'd got messed up with drugs and dropped out. Some fifteen or so years later, as a deputy sheriff, he had recognized the bruised and bloody boozer who'd been thrown into his neat, ruffle-curtained jail on a D and D.

"Man, you are *dumb*, you know what I mean? I mean you are *real dumb!* I used to think you was a real butt-head on account o' being one o' them country-club types from over'n Buena Vista, but I didn't push it, man. I mean, hell, you couldn't help it if your old man was loaded any more'n I could help it if my old man come home knee-walking drunk ever' payday of his life. That's the breaks, I figgered."

"Yeah, well—good seein' you again, too, Moose. How much you charge for a drink in this place?"

Jake had been lucky the guy hadn't dismantled him on the spot. Instead he'd done worse. He'd had his wife, a corn-fed, gingham-upholstered type, bring him over a breakfast tray that had made him sick just to smell—sausage, ham, eggs, pancakes and coffee. After Jake had finished off the pot of black coffee and covered the obscene feast with a napkin, Moose had started talking. About responsibility. About religion. About setting an example for those less fortunate.

Jake had let it roll over his head. It had been all he could do to keep from puking his guts out.

"Now you take me," the creased and spit-polished deputy had said self-righteously. "I got in trouble, and it was my own dumb fault. But I straightened up, man. I got my GED and went to Forsyth Tech, and then I met Nancy Louise and started going to church."

Jake had made some snide remark that he had regretted a thousand times since. He hadn't listened to Moose's sermon, but some of it must have sunk in. A week later he had signed himself into purgatory.

Once he'd dried out and started on the long, slippery climb back, women had been the least of Jake's worries. After winding things up in Virginia, he had moved down to Raleigh and enrolled at State, and eventually moved back to Winston. With both his parents gone by then, there had been no real reason to stay away.

Somewhere along the line it had occurred to him that he wasn't yet quite dead below the belt. He had taken a look around him, considering the odds, but as he'd never particularly cared for the game of Russian roulette, he had simply dug in his heels and worked harder. Worked until he could sleep without dreaming. Or at least dream without weeping.

How many years had it been now? Four? Closer to five. Five years without a drink, nearly that long without a woman.

And then he'd had to run afoul of that damned reunion thing and a woman named Libby Porter! He was beginning to harbor the unwelcome notion that sex just might no longer be all he needed, or even all he wanted, from a woman.

Absentmindedly massaging his temples, he muttered, "Keep it simple, Hatcher. Stick to the basics. You want a woman? Okay. Nothing strange about that."

But a lot had changed over the past few years. It was a different game now.

On the other hand, Libby Porter didn't strike him as the kind of woman who played around. She wasn't some round-heeled bimbo out for a good time. They'd been classmates, after all. She had mentioned having grown up in the house where she was currently living. It had once been part of a small dairy farm. You couldn't get much more wholesome than a dairy farmer's daughter, could you?

Jake's family was vintage Stratford Road. When he'd opted out of returning to prep school for his junior year, his family had grudgingly agreed to allow him to finish at Reynolds High. Society Hill, as it had been called in his parents' day... probably still was.

Jake had had other ideas. He hadn't been about to attend any school where he'd be a year and a half behind everyone else, where most of his classmates would be the younger brothers and sisters of the kids he'd grown up with. At least out in the county he could start fresh, without dragging a whole lot of personal baggage along with him. He'd chosen West Forsyth. His father had pulled a few strings, and Jake had commuted those last two years on his 750 Norton street bike. His family hadn't been too happy about it, but as in most things, they had let him have his way.

The Healy name had stood for something in those days, even in a town built on tobacco money, underwear money and just plain old-fashioned money. A few generations ago a local chemist named Urias Jacob Healy had mixed up a little something for a neighbor in the back room of his Fourth Street pharmacy that cleared up poison ivy practically overnight. Thus was a dynasty born, a fortune made that each succeeding generation of Healys had multiplied.

To old Urias Jacob's simple five-percent aqueous solution of a common chemical was added color, odor and a clever advertising campaign, and the next generations had prospered exponentially.

It had been Jake's father who had branched out into cosmetics. Using the family's pharmaceutical skills and the very best advertising firm money could buy, he had started out with Healy's Essence of Lotus Cosmetiques. Later, sniffing the wind, he had shifted gears and thrown everything behind a new line. Ms. T. Pharmaceuticals, named for Jake's mother, Tansey, had catered to a new breed of women who were cleverly conned into believing that the foundation of power dressing was a line of toiletries with a new name and a crisp, almost masculine new scent.

At Tansey's death, the old man had lost heart. He had followed her in less than two years, but before he had died, he had broken with tradition enough to sell the firm to a Japanese consortium, give each of his three children a million dollars seed money with no strings attached, and then he had donated the rest to various charities.

Jake's older brother had invested in a jet plane. He had died when he and his new toy had crashed somewhere over the Pacific. His sister, Eleanor, was living in Colorado with husband number three, their combined nest eggs having built a popular ski resort.

Jake, the youngest, had chosen to build his empire in Virginia, away from the influence of the Healy name. He had married a Richmond debutante, and with the ink barely dry on his degree in chemical engineering, he'd gone into plastics, elaborating on a technique of injection molding and adding certain innovations along the way. Between the toy manufacturers, optical-frame makers and a few choice government contracts, he had multiplied his seed money a dozen times over by the time his own son had been five years old.

Jake closed his eyes. A soft groan emerged from the hard line of his lips. *Johnny, Johnny...*

The shrill purr of the phone pulled him out before he got in too deep, and he lunged for it. "Yeah, yeah, whaddya want!"

He could practically feel the throb of reaction on the other end. Briefly he regretted his loss of control. "Sorry. This is Hatcher," he said in a growl that was only marginally less rude.

He heard a sigh, and then a quiet hum. Whoever the poor devil was, he'd lost his nerve. Jake couldn't much blame him. It was...what the hell, it was five minutes past midnight! Whoever the bastard was, he deserved being chewed out! And if it happened to be one of his old drinking buddies from Virginia who had tracked him down and wanted to resurrect the good old days, so much the better.

That had happened a couple of times. People he'd known in the past. Not the good past, but the past after they had lost Johnny. After Cass had left him. After Jake had seen the bottom of too many bottles and too many bars, not to mention a few select jail cells.

The phone rang again, and before he could speak, a breathless voice blurted, "Jake, I'm sorry, but I think I must have left my glasses in your car tonight. Would you please look in the morning, and if you find them, could you please leave them somewhere for me?''

"Libby? You don't even wear glasses. What's this really about?''

"I do so. That is, I wear contacts, but I always carry my glasses in case I have to take them out. I—my purse must have come open when I was—at any rate, they must have fallen out. I hope they're in your car, because if they're not, I don't know what I'll do.''

"Hang on, I'll check and call you right back.''

"You don't have to—yes, would you, please? I need to know whether or not to lie awake all night worrying.''

Jake heard the small catch in her voice, part laughter, part sob. Damn her, anyway, for getting to him this way! He hung up after promising to call her back in five minutes. Within four he was back inside, the needlepoint case in his hand. Curiously he slipped out the contents and examined them. Old habits die hard. One of the first products his plastics company had turned out in that other life of his had been frames. Top-of-the-line plastic frames, wood-grained, leather-grained, designer styles and colors.

These were rimless, wired across the top, lightly tinted and thicker on one lens than the other. The lady had herself one hell of an astigmatism, he mused as he held them up before his own eyes.

He dialed the number she had given him. "Libby? Got 'em. No, you didn't step on them, they're fine. Shall I drop them off on my way out of town in the morning?''

"I don't want you to go out of your way. Are you taking I-40 out of town?''

He was taking 421. "Yeah, sure.''

"East or west?''

"West. Shall I bring them on by?" It would mean a slight detour, but what the hell.

"Um . . . well, there's this grocery store near the Clemmons exit where I do most of my shopping, so if you could just leave them there with the manager, I can pick them up."

Clemmons was almost as convenient to 421 as it was to I-40. Libby named the store, and Jake said he'd drop them off first thing. He pressed the disconnect button in the middle of her slightly incoherent thanks and then continued to stare down at the receiver, cursing her in a halfhearted way for doing it to him again.

Damn! When the sound of a woman's voice over the phone could turn him on this way, he was in pretty bad shape. A woman with an astigmatism! A woman whose hair was grayer than his own. A woman whose right central incisor lapped ever so slightly over the left one, making him want to feel it with his tongue.

Making him want to feel *her* with his tongue . . .

Oh, geez, if this was what too much celibacy did to a man at forty, he wasn't sure he'd ever make it to forty-one!

As the crow flew, Libby's supermarket was about halfway between a job Jake's firm had recently bid on, and his office north of town. Her house wasn't that much farther out. If they landed the Davie County job, he'd probably be out in her neck of the woods pretty often.

Jake was a big-iron man. Having hit bottom after losing first his son, then his wife and then his business, he'd started the long climb back by getting another degree, this one in mechanical engineering. A few years ago he had sold a tract of land he owned in the mountains, moved back home and bought into a heavy-construction firm.

His partner, Bostic Clodfelter, was a sixty-one-year-old widower with a daughter living down in Mobile, Alabama. The two men had spent two weeks together in a fishing shack on a deserted island off the coast, where primitive didn't begin to describe the life-style. Once back in civilization, they had both been ready to sign the partnership papers with no further discussion.

Since then they had been expanding slowly but steadily. When the federal highway bill had been signed, they had added half a million dollars' worth of equipment to their fleet of heavy metal in readiness.

Jake dropped off Libby's glasses on Monday. A few hours later he was on the site of the first of three jobs they were considering bidding on. After only a brief inspection of the terrain, he turned thumbs down. He didn't like blasting, not on these grades. With a minimum of 800,000 cubic yards of dirt to be moved, most of it granite or shale, the wear and tear on the equipment would cut too deeply for comfort into their modest profit margin. Four percent they could live with. Even three. On a job like this, with the additional equipment they would have to rent, it would be closer to two.

On Tuesday afternoon he checked out the next project. Short span bridge, closer to home. They could probably handle it without having to transport the big screed by using preformed components and bringing in the small crane. This one was worth sending Mac's crew in for a tighter estimate.

There were two more possibilities, one of which Jake judged worth the time and expense of working up a bid, the other he considered too hazardous for any crew that wasn't half mountain goat. Their crews were used to working the Piedmont and points east, not west in more mountainous terrain.

By the end of the week, Jake had finished up the pre-
liminaries. He'd figured six days, told Libby two weeks,
and done the job in less than one. He stayed over another
day in an effort to convince himself that he wasn't rush-
ing back on her account.

He wanted to call her the minute he hit town, but because he was so damned hungry for the sound of her
voice, he didn't. Not the first night, nor the second one.
Monday, he figured. Or even Wednesday. He'd give himself a decent cooling-off period, and maybe on Wednesday night he would call her and see if she wanted to go out
somewhere and eat.

But after laying out his plans with the cool precision of
an experienced engineer, Jake found himself going out of
his way to shop at her grocery store. It was downright
disgusting! He never shopped for groceries more than a
couple of times a week. He wasn't that particular what he
ate. Most of the time he ate out, anyway.

On Saturday he picked up milk. He drank a lot of milk.
On Sunday afternoon, he realized that he was practically
out of bread. He might want to make himself a sandwich
at home instead of going out every night. On Monday,
when he was supposed to be working up a set of figures on
the Hopkins Hill job, he was tilted back in his office chair,
twisting a pencil between his thumb and forefinger as he
stared at the intricate shadow cast by a chart rack and the
corner of a filing cabinet.

What the devil, she wasn't all that special, he told himself. He could take her or leave her, so why not just take
her and be done with it? What did he have to prove, anyway?

Okay, so he happened to have an addictive personality.
He'd kicked booze, hadn't he? He'd kicked cigarettes, and
if he had to, he could damned well kick Libby. Figura-

tively speaking, of course. There was no way he'd ever get hooked on her. That part of his life was over. That part of him was stone cold dead.

So where was the danger? All he had to do was keep it light. Keep it on the surface. Hell, she probably wasn't looking to get involved again any more than he was!

Wednesday, he figured. He'd wait until Wednesday and give her a call. Her place or his, wherever she was more comfortable. He shouldn't have to spell it out for her.

At five-thirty he was halfway home when the craving for Moon Pies hit him out of the blue. A staple commodity, they could be bought in most every convenience store in the southeast portion of the United States, but Jake had a hunger on him for a Moon Pie from a certain supermarket near Clemmons. Before he could begin to question the urge, he was headed into the sunset along with the usual clog of going-home traffic.

Her station wagon was the first thing he saw when he pulled into the parking lot, and he nearly creamed a Honda. Deliberately he made himself circle the lot twice before he eased into a vacant slot and switched off the engine.

Now, what was it he was out of? he asked himself as he clicked the ring full of brass keys as if they were worry beads.

Oh, yeah. Milk.

She was browsing the produce, a battery of fluorescent lights glinting on the familiar crop of silver-gold hair. She did the cookie aisle, and Jake grabbed a bag at random. He followed a discreet two rows away while she finished loading her basket and took her place in the checkout line, and then he eased in behind her, feeling unaccountably vulnerable. His basket held a bag of cookies, a can of succotash, a pouch of Red Man tobacco and a box of pink tissues.

While Libby shuffled through a thick wad of coupons, Jake admired her hair. Thick and glossy, it fell straight as rain to her shoulders. Cassie used to go every two months for what she'd referred to as a body perm. He'd eventually discovered that it was something she did to her hair, not her body.

He glared at the back of Libby's head. Dammit, didn't she even know he was here? He was close enough to see the mole on the back of her neck, and she didn't even know he was here!

"Libby? I thought I recognized you."

Coupons scattered like a covey of quail. Jake retrieved a handful from the floor and handed them over.

"Jake, what on earth are you doing here?" she cried when she'd fished the rest out of her basket. "I thought you were out of town!"

"Nah, I got back a few days ago."

Why didn't you call me? The words hung between them like smoke from a skywriter's tailpipe.

"I, uh . . . hey, this is a nice store. I, uh . . . needed some milk."

She laughed, sounding as if she'd just run all the way up a down escalator. Breathless. "Me, too. That is, milk and everything else. Why do I keep hearing that inflation's so low? I know this was cheaper last week." She held up a bottle of dishwashing detergent.

"It's cumulative. Why not use paper plates?"

"The ecology."

"You could always eat out. The restaurant industry would appreciate the patronage."

"My budget wouldn't."

"You know what they say."

"What who says?" The woman in front moved out and the clerk began unloading Libby's basket. Jake realized that he'd forgotten to get the milk he'd come for.

"I don't know who said it, come to think of it, but I know I've heard it."

"Heard *what?*" she demanded with a soft little chuckle that trailed cool fingers up and down his spine.

"That two can eat as cheaply as one."

"I wouldn't be too sure of that."

Before he lost his nerve, Jake dived into the opening he'd created. "Okay, so why don't I grab us a couple of steaks, steal a couple of potatoes out of your basket, and we'll go to my place and test the theory?"

He watched while her crooked incisor sampled the soft pink flesh of her lower lip, watched a pair of lines form between her eyebrows and made himself resist the temptation to smooth them away.

"I've got all these perishables," she said, gesturing, and obediently, he glanced at the groceries the clerk was unloading onto the scarred conveyor belt. Ice cream. Ground beef. Milk. Chockie Bears. Cap'n Crunch.

Chockie Bears? Cap'n Crunch? A six-pack of apple juice?

But it was the Flintstone vitamins that did it. Warning bells began clamoring inside his head. Jake felt the very beginning of panic. He stepped back, bumped into a cart with a kid in the basket and mumbled apologies, staring at the childish treats as if they had suddenly sprouted horns. "On second thought," he mumbled, "I, uh— my—that is, I think my sink's clogged up."

"I've got a knack with clogged pipes."

"Yeah, well—the super—that is, I'd better get back. Maybe another time."

"You could come home with me. My sink's not clogged. I'd planned spaghetti tonight, but I always make enough for a platoon."

"Thanks, but no thanks. Oh, gee, would you look at that! I forgot the milk. Excuse me, Libby—lady—" Like a cornered rat, he deserted the checkout line, leaving his cart blocking traffic, leaving Libby and the strange woman staring after him. Ducking around a pyramid of canned pineapple, he hurried to the far end of the store and leaned over the meat display. His eyes were closed, but he saw with painful clarity a blue plastic bowl with yellow rabbits around the rim and a pool of milk and soggy cereal spreading out around it. His face twisted as he heard the childish voice asking, "Daddy, why is milk always blue when it spills?"

"Jake? Jake, are you all right?"

Drawing a deep breath, he opened his eyes and stared down at the small, callused hand on his sleeve. "Yeah. Yeah, I'm fine, Libby. I just forgot to pick up..."

No. No more lies! When a man reached the point of lying about his grocery list, it was time to pull out.

"Jake, why don't you come home with me? You can watch the news while I make the sauce—I cheat and use bottled, but I add stuff. It's good."

"Honey, I'm sure it is, and you're kind to ask, but I'd better pass it up. It's been a long day and I've got a lot of catching up to do. You understand."

Her eyes said she did. Said she understood all too well. Jake watched her turn away, her chin—that stubborn, elegant, angular jawline of hers—saying what she was too proud to say in words.

Oh, hell, he'd hurt her feelings. That had been the last thing he'd meant to do. Whatever he'd meant—whatever he'd intended, he had never wanted her to be hurt by anything he said or did.

Crossing his arms, he leaned against the cold metal rim of the meat counter, blocking the pork chops until the woman reaching around him for two center-cuts muttered a rude remark.

By the time Jake got outside, Libby was already gone. He pulled out into traffic and found himself turning southwest instead of northeast. The least he owed her was an apology, he told himself.

Four

Jake didn't take time to consider what he was about to do. There was something between him and Libby. Whether he wanted it or not, it was there. Once he'd had a steel splinter lodged in the thumb of his heavy work gloves. The thing had been impossible to find, even with a magnet, but it had irritated the very devil out of his thumb. He'd finally ended up throwing away a brand-new pair of horsehide gloves to put an end to the constant irritation.

He should have ended it right there at the supermarket. There was no reason on God's green earth for him to go after her. The trouble was, he was no longer running on reason. He was running on libido. He was running on sheer gut instinct.

A short time later, Jake pulled up behind her wagon just as she was unloading her sacks. She turned and waited, not smiling—looking almost wary. Then, reaching past the tailgate, she hauled out a bag and settled it on her hip. It was the one with the kids cereal on top. Jake told himself he could handle it.

Yeah, right. The way he'd handled it in the supermarket. He'd taken one good look at her groceries and hit the panic button.

"Hello again. Change your mind?" she asked, and briefly Jake considered making some excuse about noticing that she had a low tire or needed a valve job. It still wasn't too late.

It was too late. It had probably been too late the first time he'd ever laid eyes on her.

And then it hit him. The first time. It hadn't been the reunion, it had been ... "Raleigh, wasn't it? About seven or eight years ago? Some fund-raiser or another?" He lifted the sack of groceries from her arm. Through the wreckage of his past, a memory came back to him. "You wore a black velvet tent with a big white organdy bow on the shoulders, and you were sitting at a table with Charlie Alderholt and the Porters."

Porter. Her name was Libby Porter!

Jake winced at his own stupidity. Two engineering degrees, and he was about as sharp as a Ping-Pong ball.

"Jake, are you feeling all right? Why don't you come in the kitchen and sit down while I unload this junk, and then I'll make us a pot of coffee." She leaned inside the station wagon again, and watching the way she moved, the way she looked, Jake wondered why he hadn't tumbled before. Wondered why he didn't get the hell out while there was still time. Wondered what there was about this one woman that kept drawing him back like a five-dollar yo-yo.

Hell, she wasn't even all that outstanding. Strictly speaking, her hips were too wide for her waist, her jaw too firm for that swan's neck of hers, and as for her smile ...

Okay, so she had a great smile, but other than that, what was so special about Libby Porter? He could take or leave a dozen Libby Porters, any day of the week.

She emerged with the last sack of groceries and nodded toward the house. "You looked so awful in the store I hated to leave you there alone. Are you feeling better now?"

He held open the screen while she fumbled for her key. "Migraine," he mumbled, wondering just when he had turned into a chronic liar. "Used to have 'em a lot. Haven't had one in over a year." That much, at least, was the truth.

Jake still wasn't quite sure why he was here. Okay, so he'd been mildly attracted to her. She was a spur in his glove, an itch he'd considered scratching. But that was before he knew she had a kid. Before he'd remembered where he'd seen her before, pregnant as a pea pod. That particular kind of involvement he didn't need.

There was a coloring book under the kitchen table, a couple of toy trucks over near the refrigerator, and half a dozen of those bright colored plastic cubes with the holes and pegs on them. Johnny had had a bushel of the things. Jake used to step on them barefoot and threaten to hide them unless Johnny picked them up after he finished playing with them.

"Jake, why don't you—" she began, when he turned on her.

"You've got a kid," he said flatly.

Carefully removing a box of vermicelli from one of the sacks, she nodded slowly. "Yes. His name's David."

"Why didn't you admit it right up front?"

Libby's eyes glinted green fire. Up went the chin. "Admit it? Is having a child some sort of crime in your book?"

"It might've kept me from wasting my time, that's all."

He watched her pressure gauge shoot up into the red. "Well, now you know, so please don't feel like you have to linger."

"Dammit, Libby, listen to me! If I'd known—"

"No, you listen to me, Jake Hatcher!" She slammed the box down on the counter with no regard for the contents, and Jake winced, his nerves feeling every bit as fragile as the shattered vermicelli. "I didn't ask you to come barging into my life like a blasted steamroller! Not the first time, not the second time, not *any* time! That was your idea!"

"Yeah, well, it was a lousy one!"

"Then why don't you leave? I certainly don't need you. I didn't need you that night of the reunion, when that drunk made a pest of himself. I could've handled him easily enough."

Jake leaned against her refrigerator, crossed his arms over his chest and closed his eyes, waiting for her to finish blowing off.

"And I certainly don't need your permission to have a son!"

"You remember that night, too, don't you?"

"Remember what night?" she snapped.

"The first time we met."

"I don't remember anything! At least I didn't until you mentioned it. Oh, maybe I did, sort of, but I thought it was from school," she admitted grudgingly. "Your picture's not even in the annual, though," she accused. With a bunch of carrots in one hand and a bag of green beans in the other, she was leading with her chin again. Some people never learned, Jake thought.

He felt tired. He felt drained. But oddly enough, he no longer felt quite so defensive. "I remembered you, Libby, but not from twenty years ago." His eyes searched her face as if looking for all the changes the years had brought...and finding them. "From the fund-raiser. I remember one extremely pregnant woman wading through the crowd. It was raining that night, and I followed you out to the lobby, thinking you belonged to Charlie Alderholt, remember?"

Her eyes met his and glanced off. "You found me a cab. I—I had a headache and decided to leave early. If I forgot to thank you then, thanks, Jake. Now I think you'd better leave."

Caught up in remembering the rainy March night, remembering the touching mixture of fragility and determination that had caught and held his attention, Jake didn't move. He had wondered at the time why her husband wasn't looking after her.

Now he knew. No wonder she had looked so sick.

They were both still caught up in the same seven-year-old memory when somewhere in the house a door slammed. A childish voice called out, "Mom! Can Jeffie and me—"

"Jeffie and I," Libby corrected automatically, her gaze still on Jake's face. She saw—thought she saw—a stricken look in his eyes just before a familiar stoniness sealed off all expression.

The boy was small for his age. Dark. Wary. He looked like Porter, but he had a lot of his mother in him, too. The attitude, for one thing. That damn-your-soul tilt to his chin. At the moment, he was scowling up at Jake, and Jake realized that he was scowling right back. He fought down a surge of resentment.

David sidled closer to Libby and grabbed an armful of thigh, his eyes never once leaving Jake's face. Libby's fingers combed through her son's hair, and it occurred to

Jake in that instant that he couldn't recall ever having seen Cassie touch Johnny in a simple spontaneous gesture of affection.

He was hurting. Still, he made an effort to smile. It wasn't the boy's problem, it was his own, and it was time he learned to handle it. "So this is your son," he said.

Great. He sounded about as friendly as a No Trespassing sign.

"This is David. David, say hello to Mr. Hatcher."

"I don't like him, Mama," the boy muttered.

Libby flushed a dull shade of magenta. She knelt and gripped the tiny shoulders, and David ducked his head, peering resentfully out of the corner of his eyes at Jake. "David, I want you to apologize to Mr. Hatcher right now. He's a guest in our house."

"Don't want him here." His eyes were dark green, like his mother's. They were rapidly filling with tears, and Jake felt something tearing apart inside him, leaving jagged, painful edges.

"Jake, I'm sorry," Libby said quietly. She stood, with the boy leaning on her. "David usually has better manners than this. Go to your room now, David, I'll speak with you later."

The small face crumpled and burrowed into Libby's belly. Jake felt like two cents' worth of dirt. The kid spun away with one furious last look at Jake, and slammed the door behind him, and Libby's shoulders drooped. She sighed. "I'm sorry. You can see now why I don't invite men home with me."

Jake's eyes frosted over as he followed the familiar course of allowing anger to replace old feelings of guilt and grief. "I guess I can't. Why don't you tell me?" he said, deliberately stoking the anger. Anger he could handle. Anger was easy.

Libby was running water over a sink full of vegetables. "David still misses his father," she said. "Walt—that's my ex-husband—"

"I know who Walt is, remember? He's a self-centered, amoral jerk."

Libby's head came up, a look of surprise on her face. "You know him?"

It was a telling remark, and Jake felt his trumped-up anger begin to dissipate. It wasn't Libby's fault that he had a thing about kids. About the kind of ties that could choke the life out of a man. But just in case she'd misunderstood what he'd been offering her, it was time he set her straight.

No, dammit, he didn't have to set her straight, because he'd never offered her anything! "Look, I'd better be running along, Libby. It was nice seeing you. Maybe we'll do it again one of these days."

"I doubt it."

Jake was in no mood to deal with either the proud tilt of her head or that vulnerable look in her mossy-green eyes. He shrugged and took out the keys to his truck, fingering them restlessly. "Hey, look, you know how it is," he said, covering guilt with a handful of empty words. "Some men, once they hit forty—"

"Yes, I know. You don't have to explain."

No, he didn't, Jake told himself as he strode out to his truck. She probably knew better than most women what damned fools men could make of themselves, at forty and any other age.

A week later, Jake found himself back on Idol's Dam Road. He'd been in the vicinity, and with no conscious decision, he turned off toward Libby's place with nothing in mind other than seeing that she was all right. He had no intention of getting involved. Still, she was alone out there. Sometimes a woman alone needed a helping hand.

Yeah, right. Saint Jake to the rescue!

He hadn't deliberately chosen the middle of a school day, but he was just as glad the kid wouldn't be there. Jake had done some heavy thinking over the past few days. He had reached several conclusions, conclusion number one being that the world was full of kids. They were everywhere you looked, and there wasn't one damned thing he could do about it.

Conclusion number two was that he wouldn't have wanted it otherwise. If something had happened to him, and Cass and Johnny had been left behind, he wouldn't have wanted them to give up on life, to live without men in their lives. Johnny would have needed anther father, someone to help him grow up.

As for Cass...

Not in a long time had Jake allowed himself to think about his ex-wife. It was painful, guilt and anger being no small part of that pain. It wasn't until after Johnny's death that he had learned the full extent of her infidelities. Learned that she'd been in the habit of meeting her lovers at the beach—had, in fact, planned to meet one there that last time, which was why she'd locked Jake into attending the fund-raiser so he wasn't able to go with them.

Cass had planned to leave Johnny at home with the live-in nanny, but the woman had come down with the flu at the last minute, and she had hired a neighborhood teenager to look after him at the beach while she met her current lover.

Jake should never have permitted her to take the boy without Mrs. Raye, who was more of a mother to him than Cass had ever been. Jake's only excuse was that he had been busy. He had deliberately stayed busy, throwing himself into his work, trying desperately to keep from facing the fact that his marriage was falling apart.

But the thing that hurt worst of all, even after seven years, was knowing that it had been his own phone call that had caused his son's death. Jake had wanted to speak to Johnny, to assure him that Daddy would be there the minute he could get away. They'd been out on the beach, Johnny and the sitter, and hearing the phone, the girl had dashed inside to answer it, cautioning Johnny to stay right where she left him.

By the time she'd gone back outside, it had been too late. From the tiny footsteps, they figured he'd been following a sandpiper, or maybe a ghost crab, had strayed too close to the surf, and a wave had caught him, washing him out to sea.

One brief moment, and Jake's world had come to an end. Bright blue eyes, yellow curls that Cass had wanted to cut, and he had wanted to keep—that inquisitive, delightful child's mind, gone. Forever extinguished.

"Daddy, why is milk blue when you spill it and white when you drink it?"

"It has to do with the breakdown of light, son—with small particles that filter out certain frequencies—uh, colors—"

"What are par'cles?"

Jake was sitting in the company truck, parked in her driveway when Libby saw him. If she hadn't recognized those brawny shoulders in the leather jacket, the shape of his head, the way he sat with one muscular forearm draped across the top of the steering wheel, she might have taken him for a meter reader or some other utility worker in the neighborhood.

"Jake? What are you doing sitting out here by yourself?"

"Nothing, I—hello, Libby." He heard the warming of his own voice and began mentally buckling on armor plate. "I just happened to be working in the area, and I thought I'd stop by and see if you were okay."

"That's nice," she said, still sounding puzzled. "Won't you come in for a cup of coffee? I made some soup—it's nearly noon, if you're hungry."

"No thanks. I guess I'd better run along, but thanks all the same."

So why was it that a few minutes later Jake found himself seated at Libby's kitchen table, hands freshly washed, sleeves turned up to hide the grease stain on his right cuff from where he'd been checking a balky fitting on the Dynapac?

The first time he had ever laid eyes on her—a pregnant, miserable stranger across a crowded room—she had made an impression on him. The next time he'd seen her had been seven years later, in another city, another setting. He hadn't remembered her, not really, yet there'd been something about her that, rational or not, had reached out to him.

But Libby in her own kitchen was something else again. And it was that something else that was making Jake more uneasy by the minute.

It wasn't the kitchen. That was about as ordinary as they came. Brick-pattern vinyl floor, yellow enameled cabinets, circa 1930s, mason jars of sprouted vegetables in the windowsill—carrot tops, turnip tops, a sweet potato vine.

No, it wasn't just the kitchen, and it wasn't just Libby, either. It was the combination of the two that made him feel as if he were juggling sticks of dynamite on a short fuse.

She was wearing a pink cotton jumpsuit and a pair of grubby sneakers. Hardly seductress equipment. She smelled like soap and spice, and her hair, as usual, was obligingly obeying the laws of gravity by sliding out from under the red bandanna she had used to tie up her pony-tail.

Jake told himself he was being foolish. No man could be this turned on by Betty Crocker in pink coveralls. How could anything so sweet and wholesome be so damned sexy? Who'd have guessed that the smell of soap and gingerbread and chicken soup could act as an aphrodisiac? That was hitting below the belt. Literally!

Jake had been raised in a twelve-bedroom house by a staff of five and a couple of absentee parents who believed children should be relegated to third-floor play-rooms, club nurseries and boarding schools. All he remembered of the kitchen was black-and-white tile floors and a dragon in a white uniform.

As for the kitchen in his efficiency, it was white and stainless steel and it smelled of pine-scented disinfectant, courtesy of the woman who came in for an hour or so three times a week. The kitchen in the Virginia house had been the best of the lot. Lots of copper stuff hanging around, blue pottery on the shelves. Cass had supervised the decoration and then turned it over to their house-keeper. Decorative, his ex-wife surely was. Domestic, she had never even pretended to be. It had been Jake who always woke up in the middle of the night to fetch a glass of milk and a cookie for Johnny whenever he had a bad dream. It was Jake who had shared his son's breakfast at the lime-washed pine kitchen table, who had baked him a chocolate birthday cake from a mix and gaudily decorated it with gumdrops after Cass had ignored his simple request and ordered a towering, spun-sugar monstrosity from her favorite bakery.

"It's my own recipe," Libby said now, bringing him back to the present. Her cheeks were flushed as she set two full bowls on the table and opened a tube of saltines. "You should see my ex-mother-in-law's cook's favorite chicken soup recipe. Gallons of cream, tons of butter and a flock of fat hens, and that's just for starters."

He hadn't come here to swap recipes. He didn't know exactly what he had come for, but it sure as hell wasn't chicken soup! But she was looking at him expectantly, and so dutifully, Jake picked up his spoon. "This is good," he murmured a moment later. "Tasty."

"Lots of backs, lots of onions and celery, a few thighs and a tiny squirt of lemon juice. David likes it with noodles."

"So he can suck 'em up."

She glanced up at him then, and he could have kicked himself. "How did you know that? Did you used to do it, too?"

"Don't all kids? Pass the crackers, please."

They ate in silence for a few minutes, and Jake found himself staring at the faint gleam of moisture on her lips...wondering if they would taste of Libby or of chicken soup.

Wondering just when he had taken complete leave of his senses.

Five

Jake left Libby's house a few minutes later in a thoroughly rotten mood. By the time he reached his office, his mood had deteriorated still further. He snarled at Alice, their quiet, efficient secretary, glared at Bostic when he stuck his bald head through the door a few minutes later, and swore when he smashed his right forefinger trying to force a balky filing cabinet slide.

"Trouble?" Bostic asked.

"The next time you buy office equipment, stay away from the secondhand places," Jake grumbled. "You ready to go over those figures for the Stokes County job?"

"Later. Alice says the copy machine's down. She's having a replacement sent over. You want to hold that finger under cold water for a few minutes, son. Take the fire right out of it."

Jake wished to hell he could cure a few other pertinent parts of his body so easily—one of them being his head.

At five past five, he placed a call to a woman he had dated occasionally since he'd been back in Winston. Gillie was an executive secretary at a philanthropic foundation, a folk music fan straight out of the sixties, a dyed-in-the-wool liberal and a nondrinker. If she'd had any idea that the foundation she worked for had been established by his great-aunt Minnie Senate Healy, Jake would have steered well clear of her, but she was a recent transplant from New York, and as far as she knew, he was simply a big-iron contractor, single, a nondrinker who could tolerate both her politics and her taste in music, in small doses.

Gillie Novatny was an extremely good-looking woman, beads and bangles notwithstanding. A product of the times, she was emancipated enough to have propositioned him on their second date, and secure enough not to be put off when he had diplomatically turned her down.

Tonight the outcome just might be different. Tonight Jake was needing something to take his mind off a certain green-eyed, gray-haired blonde with one too many barbs to her hook.

Quietly Libby cleared a space on the low table and laid the storybook down. Tired from helping her rebuild an old chicken pen out behind the house, David was sound asleep, his favorite stuffed toy in one arm. His eyes had closed by the time she'd got to the third page, and by the end of the chapter, he'd been breathing in that slow, even rate that signified sleep.

She sighed, wondering not for the first time if she had made a mistake when she'd opted to move back home. Walt might have agreed to buy her an inexpensive house, if such a thing could be found, but his name, not hers, would have ended up on the deed. What kind of security was that?

If she had stayed on in Raleigh, David might have had a few years of private school—he'd been enrolled almost since birth. But it wouldn't have lasted. Sooner or later, Walt would have found an excuse to keep from paying the exorbitant rates, and then David would have suffered the loss of his school friends as well as the loss of his home and his father.

No, it was better this way. Begin as you mean to go on. One of her teachers, a hundred years ago, had told her that, apropos of something she had long since forgotten.

So she had begun with her own old home, which was a slightly shabby farmhouse on five acres at the end of a narrow country road. It wasn't perfect, but her parents had offered, and Libby had been only too glad to take them up on their offer. There was room for David to run wild, room for her to grow all their vegetables, and it was only twenty minutes or so from where her Aunt Lula and Uncle Calvin lived in Mocksville.

She had started David in public school, and once he'd grown used to the idea that she would still be there when he came home each day, he had gradually settled in. The trouble was Libby, herself. She was simply going to have to force herself to get involved. It had never been easy, but she'd done it once and she could do it again.

The trouble with living out in the country was that she had no close neighbors. There were times, in fact, when she was in danger of forgetting that she'd been christened Libby, and not Mama.

All of which might explain why she had latched on to Jake Hatcher like a barnacle on an oyster shell, she told herself. It was an apt analogy, she decided as she tilted the

shade of the night-light and pulled the door partially shut.
Jake could be as tight-lipped and hard to reach as the
crustiest oyster. She hadn't the least notion of what was
inside that shell of his, but she'd be willing to bet it would
be something special. Something succulent, nourishing
and incredibly tender. It might be rewarding to try and pry
open his shell. On the other hand, if he didn't like children, there was no point in it. Why tantalize herself with
a taste of forbidden fruit?

Back in the kitchen, Libby set up the ironing board.
Her mother had declared her own emancipation with the
advent of no-iron clothes. Libby could still remember the
day Dulcie Dwiggins had vowed to burn her ironing board
as a sacrifice to Saint Polyester. Funny how the cycles repeated themselves, she thought, licking a finger to test the
heat. Here she was ironing again.

Here she was, dreaming again.

Sooner or later a new generation of busy women might
discover that ironing was a miserable waste of valuable
time, but chances were, they would never learn the folly
of dreaming.

Unfolding a small blue shirt, she smoothed it over the
board, picturing a larger shirt, khaki or maybe white, and
wrinkles that would release in a drift of steam hints of
citrus and sandalwood. Instead of grippers designed for
little fingers, there would be buttons and buttonholes.
Buttons that could be unfastened, buttons that would remind her of—

"Of things best forgotten!" she muttered, slamming the
iron down on its heel. Since when had she taken up fan-
tasizing? Since when had ordinary household drudgery
stirred up dreams of hard, masculine chests, narrow waists
and lean flat abdomens?

Not to mention all the rest.

* * *

Jake saw Gillie to the door of her west-end apartment, declining an invitation to come in for decaf and cheesecake. He took the crooked cement steps two at a time, his thoughts already swinging back to the dessert Libby had offered him after he had polished off two bowls of her chicken soup.

Gingerbread arms and legs. There had been a foot, too, and a head with a frontal lobotomy where a misplaced raisin had come unstuck. "I save the perfect ones for David and eat the parts that get broken off," she'd explained. "You don't mind, do you? It all tastes the same, but since he helps me make them, I save the best ones for him. David knows how many are left in the tin. I'm teaching him subtraction that way."

Jake had got the message. Libby and son were a closed corporation. He had nibbled a few more appendages with his coffee and left soon after that, asking himself why the hell he cared, anyway.

He knew the answer. He just hadn't liked it. The more he thought about it, he told himself as he stripped down to his briefs and climbed into his bed, the less he liked it.

Dammit, the woman wasn't all that special! Gillie was prettier. Probably smarter, too. She knew her way around, knew what she wanted out of life and how to get it without being offensively aggressive. Whereas, Libby Porter...

Jake tossed restlessly for the better part of an hour before he fell asleep, his thoughts skipping over the past few hours with a tall, willowy creature with startlingly black hair, who wore layered silks and handmade jewelry and smelled of some exotic musky scent, to a gap-toothed woman in faded pink cotton coveralls who didn't bother to cover her gray, and who smelled of soap, chicken soup and gingerbread men.

A week passed. Jake was spending most of his time in Davie County on the Dutchman's Creek job. More than once he'd been forced to chase off kids who thought culverts and preformed concrete barriers were dandy playground equipment.

The job was running behind schedule, and Jake had been estimating how soon he'd be able to pull the graders off for another job. It was near quitting time. Unseasonably warm for November. Leaning against the truck, he took off his hard hat, mopped his forehead and glanced at the thickening sky. The last thing they needed now was rain! Absently he patted the pocket of his khaki shirt. He'd give twenty bucks for a smoke, but he'd quit smoking about the same time he'd quit drinking. At this point, he was beginning to think a man needed a few minor vices just to keep from going over the wall.

Suddenly he came away from the truck. "Hey, what the hell do you think you're doing?" he yelled at the small, dark-haired boy disappearing into the opening of a twenty-foot length of culvert.

Libby's kid? He was about the right size, the right coloring. But Libby's place was nowhere near here. "Don't you know you can get hurt that way, boy?" Jake muttered, his long, muscular legs eating up the distance. "Out!" he ordered, reaching in to grab a fistful of sneaker-clad foot.

He hauled the culprit out and held him up by the shoulders, checking for any sign of damage. Dammit, his men couldn't be expected to baby-sit every kid in the neighborhood! This was a construction site, which meant it was one gigantic hazard! Where the hell was this kid's mother? Who was supposed to be looking after him?

About that time an older boy came panting up. Evidently he'd been hiding behind one of the big Cats. "You two boys know better than to hang around here. Where do you live?"

Eyes as round as chinquapins, the older boy, who looked to be about twelve years old, jerked a thumb over his shoulder. "We didn't steal nothin', mister, honest."

"Yeah? How do I know that?" Jake growled. Scaring hell out of these two just might be the biggest favor anyone ever did for them.

"Y-you could search us."

Knowing all too well what had drawn them to the site—what would have drawn any normal kid, Jake continued to scowl, but his heart wasn't in it. "You guys wouldn't be planning to drive off one of my Tonka Toys now, would you?"

The two kids looked at each other, glassy-eyed, and then looked back at Jake. Behind them was every boy's dream playground—dozers, scrapers, backhoe, even a TR-500 they had brought on-site yesterday for the final grading. Hell, it was irresistible. An attractive nuisance in legal terms, which meant they had to carry a fortune in liability.

"Just don't get any bright ideas," Jake warned. "You touch a single bolt on any of this equipment, and your arm's gonna fall off, y'hear me, boy?"

"Yessir, I won't. Uh...sir? How old do you have to be to drive one o' them big yellow bucket things over there?"

Somehow, without Jake's knowing quite how it happened, the three of them spent the next half hour or so making the rounds. First Jake would point out the most obvious dangers, describe them in gory detail, and then he'd plop each boy in turn up into the high seat of each machine. With visions of a battery of OSHA inspectors bearing down on him, he took the time to explain the controls, how they worked, and why no one without sufficient strength and years of training was allowed anywhere near them. Then, after having them both practically swear a blood oath never to set foot on a construction site again until they were old enough to vote, he piled them into the crew truck and drove them home, where he had a word with a harried woman who'd been searching the neighborhood for her sons.

Ah, geez, he didn't need this, Jake told himself as he drove home. Yet, oddly enough, he felt more at peace than he'd felt in years, as if somehow he had laid a few old ghosts to rest.

Drinking had been only one part of the pattern of self-destruction Jake had followed after Johnny had drowned. Cass had been smart to leave him. Grief might have brought them closer; instead it had completed the job of driving them apart. Then, having lost the most important things in his life, Jake had thrown away the rest. His business. His self-respect. On the long climb back to respectability, he had insulated himself against feeling by the simple expedient of avoiding any woman he even suspected he might come to care for, and avoiding children altogether.

So when had the change taken place? When had he lost the rest of his mind? No man with half a brain would tempt fate by grabbing for the gold ring twice in a lifetime.

But then, a man didn't meet a woman like Libby Porter twice in a lifetime, either. The boy was a complication, but Jake was beginning to think he just might be able to handle it.

He didn't bother to call first. Taking a chance, Jake drove out to her house after he'd showered, shaved and dressed in clean khakis, a black turtleneck and a denim jacket. He took the truck instead of driving his car. Ten years ago he would have worn a suit and tie. Ten years ago he'd probably have been driving something a hell of a lot showier—a lot more expensive, at least—than either the small four-by-four pickup or the modest American-made sedan.

But then, ten years ago, he'd been John Jacob Hatcher Healy, not Jake Hatcher.

Libby opened the door wearing a peach-colored chenille bathrobe with a chain of safety pins dangling from the lapel. Her hair was hanging in damp clumps around her shoulders, and her feet were bare. Behind her, some guy on a PBS channel was demonstrating a method of root grafting, while the scent of popcorn and wood smoke eddied out to meet him.

Her eyes widened. If her jaw didn't quite drop, it gave that effect. "Jake, what are you—I mean, won't you come in?"

"Am I disturbing you? I just happened to be in the neighborhood." *Yeah. Sure you did.*

She stepped back and then closed the door behind him. The smell of some exotic blend of coffee was added to that of the popcorn and wood smoke.

"Actually, I drove out hoping you'd be here."

"That was a pretty safe bet," she said with a low, thoroughly enchanting chuckle. "I still don't know why, though."

"I guess I just wanted to see you again."

Jake didn't remove his jacket right away, although the house was warm. The fire in a tiny brick-faced fireplace was smoking slightly. There was a half-empty bowl of popcorn on a footstool, an empty cup on the coffee table, and no one had bothered to pick up the assortment of jigsaw puzzle pieces, toy trucks and picture books scattered around the room.

Without apologizing for the clutter, Libby swept a book of pirate stories off the armchair and invited Jake to take off his coat. "I'll make some more popcorn. I bought this old wire popper from a yard sale last Saturday—we'd been looking for one forever. I had the fireplace opened up again after we moved in."

She was babbling, Libby told herself. No wonder he looked as if he might turn tail and run any minute now. "We used to pop corn in the fireplace when I was little. Did you do that when you were a boy?"

Jake merely looked at her. If he'd ever popped corn in his life, he didn't remember it. His mind was too busy thinking of what she would look like under that godawful peach-colored thing and the flannel gown that was hanging out the bottom.

"Take off your coat. It's hot. I forgot to turn down the furnace when we lighted the fire, and—do you take cream and sugar?"

"No cream, no sugar and no popcorn...thanks just the same."

She looked so crestfallen, he wished he had accepted the entire menu. Instead, while she hurried off into the kitchen, he wandered over to the fireplace and examined the draft lever. By the time she came back with a tray, a steaming cup of coffee and a plate of cheese and gingerbread parts, he had broken the lever loose from the stuck position and the chimney was drawing nicely. He sat down in the chair farthest from the heat and then shifted to remove a plastic rocket launcher from under his left buttock. Somehow, this wasn't the way he had pictured things when he'd decided to see her again.

"It was stuck," he murmured, watching a soft flush of color come and go on her freshly scrubbed face. "The damper." In the reflected light of the fire, her eyes looked dark as the inside of midnight. Jake found himself staring.

"I thought it was broken. Uh—do you mind having gingerbread body parts again?" Libby set the plate down hurriedly when the crisp cookies began to slide off the plate. Oh, blast! Just when she had resigned herself to forgetting all about him, he went and turned up again! How was a body supposed to settle down to the real world when temptation kept jumping out in front of her?

They sipped coffee, darting quick glances at each other. Now that he was here, Jake couldn't think of a single thing to say. He should have called first. No—what he should have done was stay the hell away!

What did he want with her? Libby wondered. The first time, which was really the second time if not the third, they had met purely by accident. She could have been a stranger and he would still have done the same thing, getting rid of that drunk for her.

And the next time? That, too, had been sheer accident. They'd run into each other at the bank, and one thing had led to another....

Oh, for heaven's sake, the man had never even made a pass at her!

So what else was new? a familiar inner voice whispered maliciously. She was hardly the kind of woman men made passes at. Walt had, but she'd been young then, with a brand-new figure and a brand-new self-image because of it. Living away from home for the first time in her life, she had felt like someone else and it had been reflected in her

attitude. Several men had asked her out on dates before
Walt, thinking she was something out of the ordinary.
Which she certainly was not. Walt had lasted longer than
the others for the simple reason that before he could discover that she was plain old Libby Dwiggins, he had asked
her to marry him, and she had accepted.

But eventually the clock had struck midnight. The ball
had ended, and now she was back at her own smoky
hearth—older, sadder, but evidently not much wiser.

"So...have you seen any good movies lately?" she
asked brightly. Then, closing her eyes, she groaned. "I
can't believe I said that."

"No. And why not?"

"No which, and why not what?" she asked, confused.

"No, I haven't, and why can't you believe you asked
that?" She was seated on the couch, her feet drawn up
beside her. Jake pulled a domino out from underneath
him, studied it a moment, and then joined her on the
couch. "My chair seems to be booby-trapped."

"Sorry. David was feeling feverish and I put him to bed
early. Usually he does a better job of picking up."

Jake had reason to doubt that, but he kept quiet. She
was obviously not much of a disciplinarian. Or maybe she
was just trying to make up to the kid for his not having a
father—which might be okay for the short haul, but not
for the long. Not that it was any of his business.

"Jake, do you realize I don't even know what you do
for a living?"

"You never asked."

"I just did...in a manner of speaking."

"Heavy metal. Big iron. I'm a contractor."

She stared at him blankly, and without thinking, Jake
reached for her naked foot and shook it gently. "Heavy
equipment. We clear tracts of land for construction, we

build roads, small bridges—that sort of thing. Raw earth and big yellow machines, that's us.''

Jake talked for a while about some of the jobs they had done in the area, all the while absently stroking Libby's foot. Gradually, so gradually neither of them was aware of just when it happened, his words dwindled off. His fingers moved slowly over the sole of her small foot, lingering in the arch, cupping her heel, exploring the shape of each toe.

Libby's breath caught somewhere between her lungs and her throat. Her eyes were round, her mouth soft. Jake closed his own eyes, rested his head on the back of the couch, and expelled a deep, shuddering sigh.

Suddenly he was burning up, and it had nothing to do with the heating system in the drafty old farmhouse. He wanted her so much he could taste it! Wanted to fold back the lapels of that shabby old bathrobe, untie her sash and then begin on the buttons of her flowered flannel nightgown.

The foot slipped from his grasp, and Libby sat up straight, not quite looking at him. ''Would you—um, like more coffee? It—it's decaf. Half hazelnut and half something I can't even pronounce.''

But even as she spoke, they both knew coffee wasn't what he wanted. Nor was it what Libby wanted. Later, Jake didn't know whether she leaned toward him or he simply dragged her onto his lap. Whichever one of them instigated the move, the result was the same. Incendiary.

She was quivering all over. Seated on his lap, her mouth was too high for him to reach easily, and so he laid her over on the pillow and somehow managed to shift his body around until everything fit just right.

More than all right!

She tasted of coffee and gingerbread with just the faintest hint of butter on her lips. Her hair smelled of wood smoke and the same fragrance she'd been wearing the night of the reunion.

Jake's loins tightened. He parted her lips with his and dipped into the sweetness beyond while his hands slowly stroked her back, soft cotton flannel against soft satin skin. Warm, fragrant, womanly...

In the small part of his brain that still functioned, he realized that it had been years since he had kissed a woman just this way. Maybe he never had. Maybe kissing was different with each woman. He'd never thought much about it before.

Or maybe it was just different with Libby.

There was the wanting—the kind of aching, throbbing need that made a man hungry to get past the appetizer to the entrée. But there was more than that. Something he could never recall having experienced before. A need to give? A need to convey something just beyond the realm of words?

Jake lifted his lips to her eyelids, traced the curve of her cheekbone, her temple, and nibbled the downy lobe of her ear. When she gasped, he allowed his lips to trail down the rim of her jaw—that stubborn, elegant, maddening jaw—and then he took her mouth again.

You're getting in way over your head, man, a voice whispered.

Jake ignored it. He found her breasts, their sensitive peaks hardening in his palm, and he felt her tremble. "Libby," he whispered hoarsely, "we won't go any farther than you want to go, I promise you."

"I want—" She sighed as he tasted the tender flesh in the curve between her neck and her shoulder. "I want..."

"Yeah, me, too," he murmured. Wanted until he was blind, drunk, wild with it. Wanted like he had never known he could want again. It didn't make sense, not at his age. Not with his record. Not with a woman like Libby.

A woman with a son.

Six

———

Libby ignored the warnings that were going off in her head like a fire alarm. Thus ignored, they gradually faded away until there was only the faintest whisper to remind her that she would be sorry, sorry. . . .

"I never imagined anything so beautiful could come wrapped in flannel and chenille," Jake murmured. With her robe lying open, he had unfastened the buttons on her gown, leaving her all but naked from the waist up.

"I'm not—" she started to say, parroting phrases she had heard too many times ever to forget them. *Did you think you were beautiful?* Walt would jeer when he wanted to hurt her. *You think you're desirable? Sorry, babe—you're not even particularly interesting.*

Libby's hands clutched at his shoulders, her eyes clinging to his. She would have died if she could have known how expressive they were. This was Jake, she reminded herself, not Walt. And she was no longer a corn-fed farmer's daughter, overweight and insecure.

Dammit, she was an attractive, intelligent, independent woman! She deserved to be admired! What's more, she *was* interesting, too!

Jake fought his own inner demons. He hadn't meant to start a conflagration. Hell, he hadn't even meant to kiss her. But he had, and then one kiss hadn't been enough, so he'd thought he would just look, maybe touch, and then wrap her up in her cotton batting again and put her back on the shelf where he'd found her.

Who did he think he was kidding? "Honey, I'm too old to be making out on a parlor sofa."

"I know," she said breathlessly, her eyes glued to the reflection in the mirror over the fireplace. Jake's wide shoulders, his muscular back bent over her. His dark head above her blond one—her pale, naked breasts, their tips jutting like dark thimbles between the square-tipped fingers of Jake's tanned hands.

It was like watching two strangers, yet more intimate than anything she had ever experienced. Drowning in the quicksand of desire, she whispered, "Jake—I think this is probably a mistake."

"I think you're probably right," he murmured, his parted lips dragging softly across her own.

Twisting his mouth on hers, he deepened the kiss, scattering the last remnants of common sense—both his and hers—to the four winds. "Ahh, Libby," he groaned a long time later, "I thought I was past the dangerous age. Evidently I was wrong." Drawn inexorably by the taste, the texture, the sweet womanly scent of her, he kissed her again, each thrust of his tongue mirroring an act that was wholly carnal.

Libby moaned. Her arms tightened around his neck, her fingers moving restlessly through his hair. Jake tried to spare her his full weight, but on the narrow cushions, it wasn't easy.

"Libby—honey, don't you have a bed?"

She shook her head, and when his kisses strayed over her chin to her throat and beyond, she protested, "Ah, Jake, no...please!"

Jake, no, please. Jake was going out of his mind with long-denied hunger. "No" wasn't what he wanted to hear, wasn't what he'd expected to hear.

But maybe it was what he needed to hear. Awkwardly he rolled off, one knee to the floor, and then righted himself to sit beside her, his breath rawly audible. When she turned onto her side to curl around his hips, he felt like shoving her away, but he didn't. Instead he reached behind him and clumsily patted her on the shoulder.

Okay, so it wasn't entirely her fault that he was tight as a drum, that his heart was going like a jackhammer. But dammit, he was too old for this! It had been more than twenty years since he'd started something he couldn't finish—something he couldn't turn off as easily as he had turned it on.

Libby lay on her side, her fists tucked up under her chin, and stared at the wilted bouquet of autumn leaves David had presented her with the day before. She felt as limp as a line full of wash on a rainy winter Monday. As a mature, experienced woman of thirty-eight, she'd have thought she would be able to handle rejection with a bit more grace.

But then, Jake hadn't rejected her, she reminded herself. She had rejected him. At least she'd been smart enough to do that much, knowing that the last thing in the world she needed at this point in her life was to fall in love again.

Suspecting that it might already be too late.

"You all right down there?" Jake asked.

Libby nodded, and then, realizing that he wasn't looking at her, told him yes, she was. And if you believe that, she added silently, you're an even bigger fool than I am.

Uncurling herself, she sat up and began buttoning her nightgown. Jake was leaning forward, elbows resting on his thighs, forehead in his hands. His breathing, if still a bit raw, was almost steady by now. She tried to ignore him, but it was like ignoring an avalanche. By the time you were aware of it, it was usually too late to escape.

Over the years, Libby had grown better at hiding her feelings. She smoothed back her hair, retied her robe, and wished she could think of something devastatingly clever to say.

Or even something halfway coherent. For some reason, she was reminded of her first kiss. It had happened during her junior year at West Forsyth, on a Tuesday just after lunch break. Mack Shaw, class clown, had caught up with her halfway down the hall. He hadn't spoken, hadn't even glanced at her, and Libby had pretended not to notice him. She'd known better than to speak first and let herself in for one of his cutting remarks.

Suddenly Mack had shoved her against the wall and smashed a dry, bruising kiss on her mouth. Before she could even react, he was racing off down the hallway, waving his hands over his head and shouting, "Touchdown! Hey, you guys owe me five bucks, so fork over!"

Memories were supposed to lose their power to hurt after so long, weren't they?

Dammit, what was the protocol for a situation like this? She'd better start reading *Cosmo* again. "Would you care for another cup of coffee?"

"No thanks. Uh, Libby—I want you to know that I didn't come here with this in mind. Seduction, I mean."

"I didn't think you had," she replied gravely. It was true. He had never given her the impression that he was bowled over by her middle-aged charms. Mildly interested, perhaps, but certainly not bowled over.

On the other hand, he was here...again. If he wasn't after her body, what was he interested in, her scintillating conversation? Her gingerbread men? "Why did you come, Jake?"

He shrugged, and she fought the urge to lay her hand against the supple muscles of his back. He had the kind of long, wedge-shaped build that narrowed down to a taut, narrow behind. In other words, the kind of body any woman with a viable hormone in her body would find irresistible.

"Jake, I'm not very good at this kind of thing, so would you please help me out?"

"Help you out how? I did offer, you know." His smile almost broke her heart it was so beautiful. Unfortunately it never quite reached his eyes.

Once again Libby sensed a deep, lingering sadness and wondered at it. It wasn't the sort of thing she could ever ask him about. "Just play straight with me, Jake, that's all I ask. I mean, you show up, and then I don't see you for a while, and then you show up again, with no notice. I don't know what you want from me. Friendship? I'll gladly be your friend, but after what just happened—I mean, that kind of thing—" She sighed and lifted her hands, palm up.

"You want it on the level, right? No games?"

"No games, please, Jake. At our ages, we're past that stage, aren't we?"

Jake had the grace to look embarrassed. "I'm beginning to think some of us never get too old to play games."

"Not me. Before I'd even learned the rules, I'd already lost the game."

Thinking of the man she had married, Jake had to agree. But then, no one had twisted her arm. Shotgun weddings had long since gone out of style. In Porter's circle, which had also been his at one time, things seldom reached that stage, thanks to the best lawyers money could buy. "Were you in love with him?"

"With Walt?" Libby leaned forward just as Jake leaned back. She stared at the tips of her naked toes, wishing she'd had the good sense to wear her slippers. "I thought I was, at least. The first time he asked me out on a date, I thought I'd died and gone to heaven. I couldn't believe he had actually asked *me*."

"Because of who he was, you mean."

"No, because of who I was." She frowned. "Oh, you mean his money. I didn't even know about that. If I had, I'd have probably still been standing there with my mouth hanging open. Jake, I never even had a date until I was in college. Even then it was a rarity."

Somehow he found that a bit hard to believe, but he would reserve judgment. She could have been a late bloomer. "You didn't know he was loaded? That's a little hard to swallow."

Libby bristled. "Well, he didn't *act* rich! And he certainly didn't look rich. He wore jeans just like everyone else, and he drove a pickup truck. He said his folks had this farm in Wake County. How was I to know it was a tax shelter? The only farmers I knew were the kind who worked fourteen-hour days and seven-day weeks."

"So Cinderella kissed her frog and he turned into a prince before her very eyes, right?"

"Wrong. Cinderella married her prince and he turned into a frog. Warts and all."

"That's what I mean by games, honey. I expect Porter wanted to be wanted for himself, not just his bankroll. It's a common failing among the more solvent members of society. You must have been pretty naive."

"For naive, read dumb as a dipping gourd. We'd been dating for about six weeks when he gave me a Cartier watch for my birthday. I didn't even know enough to be impressed. I mean, I knew it wasn't a Timex, but it never occurred to me—I mean, it was the first time any man had ever given me a piece of jewelry. I'd probably have been almost as excited if it had come from a box of Cracker Jacks."

Jake was looking at her with one eyebrow halfway up, and she said defensively, "Well, I *did* let him know how much I appreciated it. Goodness, I must have thanked him a hundred times." She glanced up at him, a smile teasing the corners of her mouth. "Poor Walt. I'm afraid he didn't get his money's worth that time. If he'd only realized that I didn't have sense enough to be impressed, he could have saved himself a bundle."

Jake shook his head. He began to chuckle. "Honey, you were ripe for the plucking. How the devil did you manage to get past puberty without learning anything? Most girls wise up before they're even out of pigtails."

"Nobody ever offered to teach me. Is it too late for makeup classes?"

Taking her small hand into his large one, Jake traced the row of calluses at the base of her fingers. He tried to picture her as she'd been at fifteen, or twenty—or even thirty. "It's probably not worth the effort," he said. "I wouldn't lose too much sleep over it, though. In all the ways that matter, you strike me as a pretty savvy lady.''

A pretty savvy lady. Libby liked the sound of that, even if she didn't quite believe it. ''I just wish I'd struck Walt that way. Or his lawyers.''

''Rough, huh?''

Wordlessly she nodded.

''How do you feel about him now? Is it all gone?''

''Not...entirely,'' she said somewhat regretfully. ''In a way, I think I'll always love him, or at least, I'll love the little boy he must have been. He told me once he was raised by a dozen servants. I thought he was joking, but now I'm not so certain.''

Jake fell silent. The same thing had happened to him, to a lesser degree. Aside from the usual social rounds, his father had enjoyed the salmon fishing in Scotland and the elk hunting in Montana. His mother did the Paris fashion-show route, and visited a couple of spas each year, one of which was in Switzerland. Jake had never been invited along with either parent. Maybe it went with the territory.

After a moment, Libby said thoughtfully, ''I guess maybe it's more like pity I feel for him instead of love. I don't think Walt can help it, even if he's aware of it. I mean, no man would deliberately choose to be such a cold-blooded bastard, would he?''

Jake laughed. Wrapping one arm around her, he hugged her to him, and then he stood, feeling considerably better than he'd expected to be feeling a few minutes earlier. He could have debated the theory of deliberate choice, but he didn't.

A few minutes later he left, wondering if the nonplayers weren't the shrewdest gamesters of all. Maybe he should have leveled with her. For starters, he could have told her his name was Healy, not Hatcher. She had asked why he kept coming back. He could have told her that he wanted something from her—he just hadn't figured out what it was yet. Or how long he would go on wanting it. He probably should have told her he had no intention of getting in so deep he couldn't get out again when it was over.

How many brownie points did a man earn for honesty?

Five days later, Jake called and asked her out for Saturday night. "Dinner? Dancing? Maybe a movie? You call the shots."

"Oh, Jake, I can't. I promised to take David to a father-son thing over in Davie County this weekend. My uncle has invited half a dozen or so single parents with their children."

"Father-son?"

"Well, except for me. And Jeffie's mother. Most of the others are from Uncle Calvin's Young Men's Sunday school class, and since he and Aunt Lula have this place over near Smith Grove with a cabin and a pond, he thought it would be a good place to get together. David's been looking forward to it so much. We'll be sleeping over."

"What about Friday night? Or Sunday?" Jake asked after the briefest of pauses. The call had been purely impulse. He had decided not to see her again, so dammit, why couldn't he just take the reprieve she'd offered him and give thanks?

Because he couldn't, that was why.

"Jake, I'm sorry. But thank you for asking me."

He hung up. "Thank you for asking me," he mimicked, his expression anything but polite. Five minutes later, he had her on the line again. "A father-son thing, you say?"

"Jake? Well, yes . . . that is, mostly fathers and sons. I explained all that."

"Yeah, sure. There'll be one other woman and a bunch of men with their sons. You told me."

"Two more women, actually. Aunt Lula will be there. And one of the sons is a little girl. Her father's not kicking up a fuss, so I don't see why I should. What are you, a militant feminist, or a chauvinist?"

"I'm neither one. I just thought you might feel uncomfortable with all those men along, and . . . well, I thought maybe . . ."

"Jake, I practically grew up there. The pond used to be stocked with bass and bluegills, and Uncle Calvin used to take me fishing there. Now it's stocked with hybrid striped bass, but fishing is fishing, and I do know how. But thank you for your concern."

"Yeah, well . . . I just thought if you—look, just forget it, okay? Sorry I bothered you. I'll see you around."

Before Libby's smile had quite faded, he was back on the line. "Listen, why don't I just sort of tag along. For the day, I mean, not for the whole weekend. Just to sort of be there if you need a hand. I mean, David might get a backlash or something, and if all the other kids have dads there, he might—well, you know. I'm pretty good with machinery."

Libby, who could take apart a spinning reel, clean it and put it back together again as well as any man, found herself smiling again. Diplomatically she agreed that perhaps it would be a good idea to have another man along, just in case.

She hung up, telling herself it was an excellent idea. In a crowd, David might get along better with Jake—with all the other men there, that was. It was only on his own turf that David got territorial. If she was ever going to have any personal life at all outside being a mother, she was going to have to help him through this stage where he saw every man as either a threat or a potential new daddy.

Half a dozen times during the week Jake almost called up and uninvited himself. He didn't, telling himself it would be an excellent test. After that business with the kids at the Dutchman's Creek site last week, he'd been doing some thinking. It was the first time he had actually dealt one-on-one with any child since Johnny. And while he would never have deliberately sought out a kid for that purpose, he thought he had handled it pretty well. He hadn't cried. He hadn't hated them both for not being Johnny. Instead he had let each one of them sit on a machine while he answered their questions, and then driven them home, all without falling apart.

He was mending. He would never get over the loss of his own son, but that didn't mean he had to go through life avoiding any kid under the age of twelve, the way he had done for the first few years.

On Friday morning he called to get instructions on how to find the place. Hearing Libby's voice again, he felt himself begin to relax, felt a kind of warmth steal over him, almost as if he'd just downed a jigger of smooth, aged Scotch. They talked a few minutes about nothing in particular, and when he hung up after promising to drive out that evening, and again on Saturday, Jake told himself the feeling was due solely to the fact that he was finally dealing with this business of kids. That it had nothing at all to do with Libby personally.

Yeah. Right. For a minute there, he almost had himself believing it, too!

* * *

Libby was struggling to pull a hooded sweatshirt down over the arms of her impatient son when Jake's silver pickup pulled up between her uncle's Buick and Bunny Binford's Camaro. She had been watching for his car for the past few hours, but of course she might have known he would drive the truck. More in keeping with the macho male-bonding purpose of the whole affair.

Everyone else had been there when she and David had arrived, and she had fully expected to feel uncomfortable, for outside of her aunt and uncle and Bunny Binford, who was David's friend Jeffie's mother, she didn't know a soul. However, one of the things she had learned during her nearly thirteen years of marriage was how to get along in a group of strangers without going into a full-blown panic attack.

"Hi," she greeted softly when Jake came within range. David took one look, glowered and dashed away, and she shrugged a silent apology. It was too soon to expect miracles.

"I brought soft drinks, hot dogs and a bunch of other junk. It's in the back of the truck." With that lean, lazy, hip-switching walk of his, he looked positively dangerous! Libby reconsidered the possibility of panic attack.

"Oh. Good," she said a little breathlessly. "I—we were supposed to catch our supper, but Uncle Calvin's helper slipped up and fed the fish this evening. Evidently they're too stuffed to rise to a lure."

Jake couldn't take his eyes off her. She was squatting beside an open canvas bag from which protruded a pair of flannel pajamas and a rag doll that looked as if it had been rescued from a landfill. In that position, her jeans were stretched tightly across her generous posterior. With a pair of scuffed and stained yellow sneakers, she was wearing a purple turtleneck, a rust-colored headband and a faded red flannel shirt. The combination should have looked like hell, but somehow it didn't.

As he reached her, she glanced up and smiled that guileless, imperfect smile of hers, and he felt the definite beginnings of a core meltdown. *Danger, man! If you're smart, you'll get the hell out of here before it's too late!* "Yeah, well . . . I brought along a spinning rod, too, just in case it's needed," he said almost apologetically.

He had brought along three rods, three reels, a stringer, a basket, a net and enough tackle to decorate half a dozen Christmas trees, having made a run on Sears's sporting-goods department the night before.

Swallowing her self-consciousness, Libby began the introductions, acutely aware of the speculative glances that followed their progress around the six-acre pond. Bunny Binford, for instance, was all but salivating before Libby had even got out the names.

"Haven't we met somewhere before? I knew some Hatchers over in the western part of the state."

"No, ma'am, I don't think so. I'm sure I'd have remembered."

Libby steered him away to meet his host and hostess, and they talked for a few minutes with the Dwigginses before Aunt Lula excused herself to carry the little girl, who was called Peanuts, into the one-room cabin where several sleeping bags had been arranged. "Poor little dumpling. Too much excitement," she murmured, openly enjoying the role of surrogate grandmother.

After Calvin had wandered away to supervise the lighting of the bonfire, Jake said, "A father-son thing, hmmm?"

"It started out that way, I think, but one thing led to another. I guess you could call it a parent-child thing."

They had reached the truck, and Jake forked out a couple of cold drinks, having declined the offer of a beer from one of the other men. They carried two sacks of groceries over to the picnic table, where Bunny was presiding, and Libby noticed for the first time that the other woman's profile resembled a young Elizabeth Taylor, except that her eyelashes were even more spectacular. Nobody with lashes that long should be so darned likeable!

This time it was Jake who steered her away, mentioning something about sorting out fishing tackle. Libby hid her surprise better than Bunny did. The other woman obviously wasn't used to being neglected in favor of fishing tackle.

"So, David likes to fish, does he?" Talk about the kid, Jake told himself. Keep your eyes, your mind, and most definitely your hands, off his mama!

"He hasn't done all that much of it. Walt only liked deep-sea fishing, and we were never invited along."

"He seems to get along real well with his uncle."

Libby nodded. "That's one of the reasons I moved back home instead of staying on in Raleigh." Her eyes were on her son, but she was acutely aware of the man beside her. She was dangerously, recklessly attracted to him. Did he know it? Probably. She'd be an open book to a man like Jake Hatcher. He was more in Bunny's league.

Instead of stopping by the truck where his fishing tackle was, Jake steered her toward a fallen log some distance away from the leaping bonfire that had just been ignited, urging her to sit and then dropping down beside her. He dug the heels of his boots into the dirt, and for several minutes neither of them spoke.

And then he said, "Libby, there are a few things you don't know about me."

Libby's fingers tightened their grip on her bottle. She focused her eyes on the sliver of a moon that was rising against the amethyst glow of sunset. She might have known it was too good to be true. He was married. He was engaged. He was destined for the priesthood. The best ones were always out of reach.

Only why had he waited to tell her until it was too late? "Look, there's the moon," she said too brightly. Whatever he was going to tell her, she didn't want to hear it.

Jake hadn't intended to tell her anything. What difference did a name make? Okay, so the second time around he had wanted to make it on his own, without the help of family connections. Where was the crime in that?

But in light of what she'd told him about Porter's approach, it suddenly didn't seem quite so harmless. Was it a game? It hadn't been intended that way. It had been purely a business decision.

Okay, it had been *partly* a business decision.

But suddenly it was important that she know who he was.

Seven

"It's Healy," Jake told her. "Hatcher's my middle name. It was my mother's maiden name."

"I know," Libby said quietly as she connected the dots she had poked in the ground with a stick.

He was thunderstruck. "You know! How the hell could you know?"

"Something Aunt Lula said about old Mr. Healy's drugstore on Fourth Street. Her mother used to work there when she was a girl, and there used to be a Miss Ada Hatcher who would come in every Wednesday morning like clockwork to get 'A Little Something For Sister.' That was the way she always said it. Aunt Lula says she remembers her, but I expect she just remembers hearing about her."

"That would be my Great-aunt Ada. The 'little something for Sister' was probably paregoric. Poppy juice in various forms was perfectly legal back in those days."

Jake shook his head and asked, "But how the devil did you connect all that to me?"

"Hatcher. There aren't that many around here. Then, too, the first time I met you...remember? Not the reunion, but that fund-raiser? It wasn't the sort of bash I'd have expected a construction worker to attend, so I looked in my high school annual again for the list of those whose photos weren't included, and there was John J. Hatcher Healy. Something just clicked."

"How long have you known?"

Libby tossed down her stick and slanted him one of her shy smiles. "Only two or three days, and I wasn't really sure even then, but my instincts are usually pretty sound."

Damn her instincts! Having finally screwed up his nerve to bare his soul, Jake was feeling distinctly deflated. It wasn't a feeling he particularly enjoyed. "What happened to your fine instincts where Porter's concerned?" he asked, and then wished he hadn't.

"I guess maybe they developed late in life," she replied quietly, making him feel even worse.

Jake began to relent. Okay, so she'd guessed about the name. But whatever else he might have told her, he had changed his mind. Talk about your instincts; one in particular was clamoring for him to get the hell out of there before it was too late. It was called survival instinct, and his had been running well into the red zone ever since the second time he'd seen her.

"But Jake, why?"

"Why what?" he grumbled. He picked up the stick she had tossed down and drew a circle around three of her dots.

"You know—the name."

He shrugged. "Hell, I don't know. Call it a business decision. It's a long jump from body lotions and after-bath splash to boom drills and padfoot rollers. No point in confusing the market.''

"I'm surprised you got away with it. You must know a lot of people around here."

"Times change. Industries, like dynasties, rise and fall. Old families die out or move away and new ones move in. Nobody pays much attention."

"What about old friends?"

The bonfire flared, sending up a shower of sparks into the still evening air. Several yards away, men were telling fish stories. Bunny and Aunt Lula were laying out the supper makings. A few boys were listening to the stories, a couple were arguing the merits of crickets over worms, and one demanded to know why he couldn't just peepee behind a bush instead of going all the way to the outhouse.

"Friends scatter, too," Jake said quietly. "How many of our mutual classmates have you kept up with over the past twenty years?"

Libby wrapped her arms around her knees and stared at the figures silhouetted against the fire. David was one of them. "None, I guess, but then I never had any close friends in high school. You must've had hundreds. You were one of those mythical figures we nerds could only worship from afar."

Relenting in spite of himself, Jake took hold of her ponytail and gave it a gentle yank. "Did you worship me from afar, Libby?"

"If I thought your ego needed it, I might tell you I did, but the truth is, I sort of had a crush on the head of the science club. You remember . . . what's his name? He had red hair and glasses and he always wore striped shirts and a tie?"

Jake laughed aloud. "Thanks a lot!"

They both fell silent, thinking of friends past and present. In Libby's case, there weren't many. In Jake's, perhaps too many... once. Money had always had a certain drawing power. Sooner or later, however, someone with more of it came along. He had spent all of thirty seconds mourning the loss of his old schoolmates, and a bit more thinking of the friends he and Cass had made in Richmond. Once things had started falling apart, they had quickly drifted away. Jake hadn't blamed them, nor had he particularly missed them.

Maybe there'd always been this element of lone-wolfishness in his makeup, he didn't know. He did know it was safer. Lonesome was a hell of a lot more bearable than having your guts ripped out.

"Although there was this one guy," he said thoughtfully. "Moose Capeheart. Must've been a year or so behind us. You remember him."

"The name sounds familiar, but I can't place him."

"Big guy. Played football. Got caught smoking the wrong stuff once too often and was kicked out."

"My goodness, they actually did that back then, didn't they?"

"Age of innocence, relatively speaking. I almost wish we could go back. Anyhow, Moose did. Go back, that is. Took a GED, wound up working in a small town in Virginia as a deputy sheriff. Maybe one of these days I'll give him a call, let him know where I am."

If Libby considered a small-town sheriff an unlikely candidate for friendship with the scion of one of the town's wealthiest families, she had better sense than to say so. Jake had his own reasons. He was a very private man. As well as being drawn to his strength, she was drawn to the depths she sensed when he was in this pensive mood.

Supper was blackened wieners, smoky, sizzling with juices, and loaded with extras. The third time Jake declined a beer, he mentioned being allergic to alcohol. After that, there were no more offers.

A sticky-faced David came and pushed himself in between Jake and Libby, and while Libby mopped him off, Jake turned to talk to Calvin Dwiggins. One of the other men, a CPA with weekend custody of his eight-year-old son, joined in, and the talk became general as one by one the children fell asleep and were bedded down inside the cabin.

Libby left with her sleepy son and returned after half an hour. "Two more down for the count," she said, "if you count Ikky."

It was only a bit past nine, but it seemed much later. The days had shrunk until night seemed to fall with no warning in the middle of the afternoon. Jake dragged their log closer to the fire, and when she sat down, he took his place beside her, draping an arm loosely across her shoulders. While Bunny Binford watched from the other side of the fire, they talked about schools, about cold remedies and about the pros and cons of aquaculture in an area this far west. Sexy, stimulating stuff, Libby thought with rueful amusement. She wished it could go on forever.

"Saline content," her uncle declared. "That's what makes it so danged tricky. We're too far east here to do much good with mountain trout, and just about too far west for hybrid stripers."

"Always fall back on catfish and carp," someone else said, and they all laughed.

Libby leaned her head on Jake's shoulder and allowed the peacefulness to seep into her bones. How long had it been since she had enjoyed such a gathering? Old friends, new ones, family—all ages from three to sixty-seven. No tensions, no axes to grind—nothing to prove to anyone. It took her back to her younger days, when she was just another little towheaded Dwiggins, one who could swim as well as any boy and fish better than most. The days before she realized that being overweight made her socially unacceptable, compounding the usual problems of adolescence a hundredfold.

"Having a good time?" Jake murmured after a while.

"Heavenly." She yawned and begged his pardon. "How on earth could I be sleepy at this hour?"

"Full stomach, long day. If you want to turn in, don't let me keep you. I've got to be getting back to town, anyhow. The mess on my desk is about two feet deep. Mostly EPA stuff. File it or face a firing squad."

Libby yawned again. "Sorry. I can't seem to stop. Wish I could just roll over right here by the fire, but I reckon my backside would freeze long before morning."

"Not if I kept it warm for you."

Her eyes flew to his and hung there. Her breath quickened, and Jake swallowed hard. Damn. So much for survival instinct.

Libby lifted her head from his shoulder and leaned forward, and Jake's arm fell away. "Did you see David watching the way you twisted that apple in half with your bare hands?" she asked quickly, her voice skittering over the words like a mayfly over the pond. "His eyes were big as saucers."

"I hope he was impressed," Jake said with a wry grin. "I was sure as hell showing off. Next time, though, remind me not to try it on one with wrinkled skin. That one must've been last year's crop."

She laughed, as she was supposed to, and Jake rose, stretched and said his good-nights around the fire. Libby watched Bunny Binford watching him, and felt a smug touch of possessiveness.

"Welcome to pull up a stump and stay over, son," Calvin invited. "I ain't offering to share my bedroll, nor the mattress in the back of my camper, but—"

"You'll share or sleep on the ground, old man," Lula shot back, and in the general laughter, Jake drew Libby toward the truck.

Away from the bonfire, the night was pitch dark except for the fingernail sliver of moon and a handful of stars. The air smelled of wood smoke, pond water and resinous pines. Nearby, a ripe persimmon plopped to the ground. Libby tried to soak up every detail to store in her memory.

"Will you come back out tomorrow?" she asked.

"Do you think it's a good idea?"

"I didn't mean—I meant, if you want to, you're welcome."

They were both fencing. Libby ached for him to come back tomorrow, ached even more for him to stay here now, but she was nothing if not a realist. Every minute spent in his company only made her hungrier for more, but she had David to think of. So far, Jake and David hadn't spoken more than a dozen words to each other, and none of those particularly friendly. Even if Jake was interested in a long-term relationship, that would be a problem.

On the other hand, if he was interested in something less than a long-term relationship, that would be even more of a problem, both for David and for Libby.

Not until they were standing beside the truck did Jake take her in his arms. Libby leaned her forehead against his chest, savoring the mingled scent of smoke, onions and Jake. It was a heady combination.

"Sure you're going to be warm enough tonight?" he growled against the top of her head.

"David's using my old sleeping bag, but I've got a quilt, a woolen blanket and a pair of insulated longhandles." How romantic can you get, she thought ruefully.

"My back-warming offer's still open."

She glanced up, laughter shining from her eyes, and Jake took advantage of the implicit invitation to lower his face to hers. Before either of them was quite prepared, what was intended as a simple, friendly good-night kiss escalated to something considerably more.

With a low groan, Jake lifted his head to stare down at the pale blur of her face. He swore softly. Libby had time only for one deep, ragged breath before he was back again, taking her mouth with a sexual urgency that shook her to her very roots. She strained against him, wrapping her arms tightly around his waist. Jake held the back of her head in one large hand while his other hand moved restlessly over her back, dropping to curve over her hips. He turned her so that she was braced against the side of the truck and then he moved even closer, straddling one of her thighs with his own, shifting his pelvis so that she could be in no doubt of what he wanted from her.

And oh, she wanted it, too! Not since the early days of her marriage had she wanted a man this much! Not even then. At first she'd been too inexperienced, and Walt had not been a particularly patient lover. The novelty of her virginity hadn't lasted much beyond the honeymoon, and by the time she had gained even an inkling of her own sexual potential, he had all but lost interest in sex.

With her, at least. She hadn't known then about the other women in his life. That knowledge had come later. Too proud to beg, and too proud to let him know how she felt, Libby had thrown herself into all the worthy activities expected of the women in her new social set. After a while, she hadn't felt much of anything.

Until now. Until Jake.

"You know I want you, don't you, Libby?" he whispered against her throat.

She shuddered at the effect his mouth had on the sensitive nerves there. Oh, she knew! But how long would he go on wanting her? For a single night? A week? A year? How did a woman find out something like that? Did she dare ask?

"Libby? Sweetheart, did you hear me?"

"I heard you," she said in a soft rush of words. "I'm thinking, I'm thinking!"

Jake laughed, and some of the explosive tension seemed to evaporate. Bumping her forehead with his, he said, "Look, why don't we just give it a little more time, hmmm?"

He had nearly said: why don't we sleep on it? Under the circumstances, that might have been construed as a double entendre. Meanwhile a few hours of filling out EPA forms would probably solve his problem—at least temporarily.

But he had an idea it would rise again the next time they were together. And that was *definitely* a double entendre!

Jake knew he wasn't going to be able to stay away the next day, which was Saturday. But first he took the time to drop by the job site. Even with no crew there, he managed to kill a couple of hours checking the condition and the security of the machinery.

Dammit, there was no point in letting any woman think she was the most important thing in his life, because she wasn't. Jake had aligned his priorities a long time ago.

About the same time he'd gone into partnership with Bostic Clodfelter, in fact. Eighty percent of him would be devoted to keeping the business in the black. Anything left over could be devoted to whatever the hell he felt like getting involved in, the catch being that twenty percent of a man's time was hardly enough to get him into any serious, long-term trouble.

At least, that had been the plan. Until lately it had worked out just fine. He had gone out with any number of women...once or twice. Gillie Novatny had lasted longer than any of the others simply because she didn't bore him to distraction after a few hours.

And maybe because he had known right from the beginning that she would never be a threat to him. Oh, she was attractive enough. Intelligent, she had a sense of humor, too. It was a bit too caustic for his taste, but they'd had a few good laughs together.

So why was it that he could see her once or twice a month and never give her a single thought between dates? Why was it that he could run into this short, hippy, gray-haired blonde in the bank or the supermarket and nearly bust the buttons off his jeans? Hell, the woman couldn't even dance! Her political savvy was no more than average. Her sense of humor was so off-the-wall she laughed in the wrong places at half his jokes—if she laughed at all.

So *why?*

Jake told himself that a man his age, a man with two engineering degrees, ought to be able to figure out a little thing like *why.* All it took was a coolheaded application of logic. An analysis of the various components.

The trouble was, where Libby was concerned, he was neither coolheaded nor analytical. All he wanted to apply was himself...to her! When a man could get turned on by simply sitting in a kitchen eating gingerbread parts, something was definitely out of kilter.

It was nearly three in the afternoon by the time he parked his pickup behind the assortment of vehicles at the Dwiggins place. Both boats were pulled up onto the bank, a trickle of smoke was coming from the chimney in the crude, one-room cabin, and half a dozen fishermen of assorted ages and genders were scattered around the banks of the pond.

Jake spotted her immediately. She was squatting down on the sloping dam, coaching her son, who seemed to have hooked into something pretty sizable. Watching the small drama unfold, he started around the pond. The boy, he was amused to note, had set his chin in a way that was purely Libby.

Jake felt a twinge of an old, familiar ache. David was nothing at all like Johnny. Neither as sweet nor as gentle. But then, Johnny had not lived to develop a seven-year-old's independence.

"Watch out for the holes in the bank," Libby called out as Jake started down the slope toward where the battle was in progress. "Between muskrats and erosion, they're all over."

"Erotic banks. Sounds interesting," he said with a grin.

"You won't think it's quite so interesting if you step in one and break a leg," she shot back. Turning her attention to her son, she said, "That's right, baby, don't give him any slack. Lift your tip, drop it, and then reel in fast! Lift, drop and reel—that's it!"

Baby? Hell, even a mother ought to know better than that. Jake's eyes met David's in an exclusively male look of commiseration as Jake paused halfway down the bank to watch. Maybe if the fish was big enough, the boy would forget what she'd called him. In public, yet!

She was doing a surprisingly good job of coaching, though. Jake watched as she reached behind her to pick up the net and move in for the kill. And then suddenly, she lurched and seemed to grow shorter before his very eyes.

Everything happened at once. David yelped and threw down his rod, Libby twisted, to tumble slowly in a graceful arc, landing flat on her back in the deepest part of the pond, while Jake skidded the remaining distance and dived in just as she surfaced again.

It was over almost as quickly as it had begun, at least as far as Jake and Libby were concerned. After several clumsy attempts, he managed to get them both back up on shore before the kid could dive in to rescue his mother. By that time, everyone was yelling something about the rod.

Jake cleared his sinuses, flung his dripping hair off his forehead and leaned forward, hands on his thighs, to catch his breath. Beside him, Libby was stretched out on the steep bank, facedown, her jeans liberally streaked with red mud and her sweatshirt plastered to her back. Her fingertips were already beginning to take on a purplish tint. It was only then that Jake noticed the cutting wind. He swore. Another few minutes and she'd be chilled to the bone, if she wasn't already.

"Mama, Mama, wake up!" David tugged on his mother's shoulder.

"Honey, let's get you somewhere warm, fast," Jake muttered. To David he said, "Your mama's just fine, son. We'll dry her off and she'll be good as new."

Eyes still tightly shut, Libby whispered a rude word. "I told you to watch your step—I warned you! And then I had to be the one to step in a blasted muskrat hole! I'm so embarrassed."

"Mama, look at my fishing pole," David cried, and she rolled over and sat up, with Jake crouching behind her in an effort to block the piercing northwest wind.

Having satisfied himself that she was in no immediate danger, David dashed off to join the rest of the company in a race to recapture his spinning rod, which was streaking across the pond, tip first.

By the time Jake herded a complaining Libby into his truck, the game was in full swing, with Calvin and David headed out in one of the boats. Everyone else was casting from the bank, trying to hook the reel. Aunt Lula, with one eye on the race, assured Libby that she would look after David while Libby got herself a nice hot shower and some warm, dry clothes.

"You, too, Jake. Oh, and would you mind picking up a couple of cans of milk and some cocoa on your way back? I promised the boys to make a panful of cocoa the old-fashioned way tonight."

Jake turned up the heat full-blast. He wasn't all that cold now that he was out of the wind, but he was beginning to worry about Libby. She was huddled up in a small knot, staring down at her mud-streaked knees as if they were the most fascinating things in the world...which they well might be. He was in no position to judge, unfortunately.

"Hey, it's not all that bad," he said softly when they had driven several miles in silence.

"Yes it is."

"So you're wet. You're washable...aren't you? You're not going to melt and get my seat covers all sticky, are you?"

"I never felt so stupid in all my life," she said flatly.

"Then you're lucky." They were crossing the Yadkin River bridge. He reached over and covered her clenched fists with his right hand. "Honey, you stepped in a muskrat hole. You said yourself it was an erotic bank. It could have happened to anyone, even me, and I'm damn near perfect."

A small sound escaped her pale lips. It was a poor effort, but Jake figured it was better than nothing. "Thanks for the rescue, anyway," she said with a sigh.

"Anyway? What does that mean?"

"It doesn't mean anything. It just means thanks for the rescue."

"'Anyway,' you said. That's like a caveat after a compliment. What did you mean, thanks for dragging me through the mud? Thanks for not laughing when my shoe came off? What, Libby? I want to know what's the matter with my brand of heroics."

By then she was giggling. Jake suppressed an urge to pull over into the emergency lane and wrap her so tightly in his arms she'd never come unwound. "Hey, it's all over, honey, with no one the worse for wear," he said softly.

"I know, but I just can't help thinking that it could've been David. Jake, what if I hadn't been there and he'd stepped into that hole? What if he falls in while I'm gone? Oh, lordy, what if—"

"Quit it. No more 'what-if,' Libby. There are half a dozen people out there to keep an eye on him. He'll be all right."

Jake knew better than most people that "what-ifs" could drive a person crazy.

The moment they pulled up in her driveway, Libby jumped out of the truck. Jake followed her to the house, and she turned to tell him when to pick her up again, but when she unlocked the door, he followed her inside.

"You've got a washer and dryer, haven't you?" he asked.

She nodded. Shivering almost uncontrollably, she wanted only to immerse herself in hot water. After that, she might be able to function again.

"Okay, then I'll toss my things in with yours. You get the first bath, and I'll use whatever's left of the hot water. I'm easy to get along with."

"Wait a minute, what do you mean you'll toss your things in with mine?"

"Libby, be reasonable. It's at least half an hour to my place, without Saturday afternoon traffic. My laundry facilities consist of two communal machines in the basement, usually either busy or out of order. You want to get back out there before dark, don't you? If so, it seems only reasonable to me to double up here."

Double up. Libby didn't like the sound of that.

Yes, she did, too! That was the trouble; she liked it entirely too much. She had enough problems in her life just building a secure future for her son without complicating matters any further. And Jake was a complication of the first order.

Knowing full well she ought to send him on his way, she heard herself saying, "David's room's right through there. I guess you can use it to change in. Throw out your wet clothes, and I'll start the washer. They can wash on short cycle during my shower and dry during yours."

So much for a deep, hot soak. She had a thirty-gallon hot-water heater that took forever to recover.

"Of course, there is an alternative, in case you're into water conservation," Jake suggested, a wicked glint in his dark eyes.

Even soaked to the skin, with his hair looking as if it had been groomed with a hay rake, he was altogether too tempting. Libby crossed her arms over her chest.

"On the other hand," he said hastily, "there's no real shortage of water around these parts."

Eight

Any other man would have looked ludicrous wrapped in a quilt, with his bare, hairy legs hanging out. Not Jake. Any other man would have had the good sense to stay put, either in the living room, the kitchen where Libby had set coffee to dripping, or in David's room.

Not Jake. He prowled. Having confiscated the quilt off the foot of the bunk bed, he padded barefoot from room to room, examining windows that needed puttying, faucets that needed washering, even discovering the matchbooks someone had jammed under the front of the refrigerator to keep the door from hanging open.

Libby paused in the doorway long enough to tell him the wash was underway and should be done in about fifteen minutes.

"I'll wait," Jake muttered.

"I didn't think you were about to take off dressed like a Roman emperor." She grinned. When she'd picked out the dinosaur quilt for David's bed, she hadn't quite pictured it serving as a toga for a strapping, six-foot-two big-iron contractor.

Jake glowered at her, and she ducked into the bathroom and shut the door. Leaning against it for a moment, she clutched her robe and dry underwear to her chest and smiled. He was so... He was just so...

She didn't know what he was. All she knew was that being around him made her feel sort of itchy, sort of achy. As if she were about to break out all over with something that would mark her for life.

Falling into the pond and having to be hauled out over a muddy bank wasn't bad enough, she thought sadly. She'd had to compound the disaster by letting him drive her home and share her facilities. Now every time she stepped into her bathtub she'd be picturing him standing right where she was standing now, sluicing down, lathering up, tilting his head to wet his hair, lifting first one arm, then the other—stroking soapsuds down over his hard, flat belly....

"Oh, lordy," she moaned, shutting her eyes against the sting of shampoo.

With some vague notion of getting him out of her house before any further damage could be done, Libby knotted her bathrobe around her still-damp body a few minutes later and hurried down the hall to the utility room. Out of the washer, into the dryer. Thirty minutes, tops, she figured, and they could be on their way.

Efficiently she sorted the small load and tossed the heaviest things into the dryer. Her jeans and sweatshirt, Jake's jeans and khaki shirt. Their lighter things could go in at the last minute—her panties, bra and Orlon socks, his navy nylon briefs and—

"Jake! What about these wool socks?" she yelled without looking around.

"What about them?"

He was so close she jumped. "I didn't hear you come in," she accused.

"I'm barefoot. Next time I'll jingle the loose change in my pocket."

Her gaze dropped to the bunk-size quilt that was artfully draped around his loins, and bounced back up again. Face flaming, she set the switch and slammed the dryer door. "Maybe they'll dry if I lay them on top," she mumbled, practically throwing the socks down in her rush to escape the confines of the tiny utility room.

He didn't budge. "If you'll excuse me," she said pointedly.

"I won't."

"Jake—" Her eyes pleaded with him as he reached out and brushed her damp hair back over her shoulders. His hands settled there, and she felt the heat of him, felt as if she were bonded to him for life. "The—the coffee should be ready by now," she whispered in a desperate effort to distract him.

"Come here, Libby." Jake wasn't a man to be distracted. It was there in the dark gleam of his narrowed eyes, in the heightened flush of his lean and angular face.

Libby wrenched herself from under his hands, and then was sorry she had. It was as if a part of her own body had been ripped away. "I—that is, we could pick up marshmallows when we stop for cocoa." The words sounded like so much gibberish. They were.

"Marshmallows. Right. I'll make a note of it. Now come here, Libby."

What choice did she have? Could the tide resist the moon? In one last desperate attempt to hang on to her soul, she pleaded, "Jake, please don't start anything foolish. It's only going to complicate things, and neither of us needs—"

"I know what I need, Libby. I think I know what you need, too."

"No, you don't! That's the very last thing I need!"

He was so close she could see the crow's-feet at the corners of his eyes, see the random gleam of silver in his dark, thick hair. "What don't you need? You don't even know what I was going to say," he purred.

But she knew, and he knew she knew. Because it was what they both wanted, and suddenly Libby was too tired to resist any longer. Yes, she wanted him! She had dreamed of feeling the length of him pressing against her, dreamed of his arms holding her through the night. She wanted to bask in his quick, rare smiles, his even rarer laughter. Wanted to share the sadness that lay buried deep inside him, and if she couldn't share it, then at least comfort him for a little while.

It wasn't love, she told herself. Jake had never pretended to love her. But whatever it was he was offering, why shouldn't she accept it? It wasn't as if she was stealing something from someone else. No one would be hurt by it. Nothing would be changed. The sun would still rise tomorrow.

His gaze never leaving hers, Jake bent and swept her up into his arms. If eyes could be said to speak, his did. And what they were saying brought a rush of heat from the soles of her feet to the crown of her head. He shouldered the door to her room open and slowly lowered her to the crocheted rug beside the bed.

Libby came down to earth, literally and figuratively, as echoes from the past rose to haunt her, bringing with them the familiar feelings of inadequacy that she could never quite manage to erase, no matter how much weight she lost or how many pretty clothes she wore.

Her self-image had been formed early. Time had diminished its spell, but nothing could banish it completely. Walt had made excellent use of it once he had discovered her secret weakness. To this day, she was uncomfortable with her own nakedness. Her breasts were too small. Her hips were too wide. He had seen better legs on a piano. He had seen to it that she felt woefully inadequate in the bedroom, unsure of her ability to please a man even for the few minutes required for the sex act.

She closed her eyes, as if not seeing could somehow make her invisible.

Sensing a certain withdrawal, Jake didn't press her. Instead he moved around her bedroom, supremely unselfconscious in his ridiculous outfit, touching her silverbacked mirror, her hairbrush and the bottle of *eau de toilette* beside David's school picture. He couldn't remember a time when he had felt so protective and so damned horny at the same time.

Of course she was nervous. He was nervous, too. But it was going to happen, and waiting wasn't going to help either one of them. Besides, dammit, just being around her lately was keeping him in an almost constant state of arousal. At his age, that was ridiculous!

The whole thing was ridiculous. Look at them—she was standing over there, studying the bedpost, and here he was on the other side of the room, sneaking peeks at her, like some steamed-up fifteen-year-old!

Objectively speaking, she wasn't even particularly pretty. He couldn't for the life of him figure out what made her so damned special. The best he could come up with was a bunch of little things. Like the way she had of lifting her chin. Like the way her hair sprang thick and glossy from a cowlick at the very crown of her head. Like the way her eyes could soften one minute, grow serious the next, and then light up with little golden sparks of laughter.

Like the way he felt when he was around her. Warm, comfortable and comforted. Accepted with no explanations asked, none given.

Rounding the foot of the bed, he reached out and touched the chain of safety pins dangling from her lapel. "Nice jewelry. Understated."

"It's for emergencies. At least this way I always know where to find one."

"Speaking of emergencies, you don't have to worry. About me, that is. If I had the least doubt of that, things would never have gone this far."

"I know that, Jake. Me, too." After learning of Walt's indiscretions, she had made an appointment to be tested. That night she had moved into the guest room. "Jake, it's been a long time for me. You may as well know that I, uh—" She cleared her throat. "I've never been very good at it," she finished in a rush.

"That's what you said about dancing," he reminded her, a teasing smile playing at the corners of his eyes.

"Yes, and I was right, too, wasn't I?"

"I thought we managed pretty well," he said as he untied the sash of her robe. "Steel-toed slippers and all."

She swallowed hard and closed her eyes against what was happening. "I just don't want you to—to expect too much."

"Let me be the judge of that." His hands moved again and her robe slithered silently to the floor.

"That's what I'm afraid of. Being judged," she said with a nervous laugh. Being judged and found wanting. Again.

The touch of his mouth in the hollow of her throat made her knees buckle. Jake caught her around the waist and lowered her onto the bed, following her down, and she lay there stiffly, afraid to move, almost afraid to breathe. Above her, Jake's face was suddenly the face of a stranger. A harsh, compelling mask that had been chiseled from stone.

Libby was too frightened by the intensity of what was happening to her to protest as he began touching her here, kissing her there—caressing her in ways that were both gentle and incendiary.

Oh, my glory, you can't do that! I'm coming apart!

But her only audible response was the catch of her breath, the occasional deep, shuddering gasp. And then, "Jake, what are you—Jake!"

"Hush, love—let me make you bloom."

Oh, oh, oh! She had never, ever gone up in flames this way before!

Desperate to hang on to a shred of sanity, Libby lifted her head and looked down at what he was doing to her.

And then wished she hadn't. If his kisses, his caresses, had set her on fire, the sight of those tanned and callused hands on her vulnerable flesh had the effect of throwing fuel on the flames.

"Help me," he ordered gruffly.

"Help you how? Jake, please—I don't know how. I'll do it all wrong."

"At least get this damned thing off me," he growled, and lifting her head again, Libby saw that the quilt was twisted around his waist like a misplaced, dinosaur-printed leash. Her lips began to tremble.

"Laugh and you'll regret it," he warned her, but when a giggle escaped her and he sank his teeth tenderly into her throat, she found that she didn't regret it at all.

Eventually, working together with several rather interesting distractions, they managed to free him from bondage. By that time, Libby had gained a considerable store of confidence. She watched openly as he moved over her, the scent of her soap and her lavender sachets mingling erotically with a deeper, more sensual note.

Including two male cousins she had discovered skinny-dipping at the pond when she was nine, Libby had seen a total of three adult nude males. Until Jake. He was magnificent, his broad shoulders still tanned from summer, the dark hair patterning his chest, leading the eye downward to—

Oh, my.

"Touch me, Libby," Jake asked, and taking her hand, he guided her. Her gaze never left his. She was trembling, but she followed his lead, and then daringly took control until Jake had to lead her away for the sake of his own sanity.

Willing himself to patience, he gazed down at the woman who lay open and trembling beneath him. There was something incredibly touching about a woman's vulnerability. Jake had never thought about it before. At this stage of the game, he wasn't usually capable of thought. Yet in that very vulnerability, he acknowledged, lay a woman's greatest strength. What man in his right mind could ever hurt something so wonderful?

Carefully he traced the fragile line of her collarbone, slipping down into the valley between her breasts, and then trailing up one pale slope to circle the dusky tip. Her nipples were dark and generous, and he found himself wondering if she had nursed her baby.

Oh, God, not now! He didn't want to think of anything but this moment, this woman. That was all that mattered. To make it good for her, because he was pretty sure it hadn't been so good in the past.

Taut with his own urgent need, Jake forced himself to draw out the tension, as if by doing so he could make it last forever.

Nothing lasts forever, a voice inside him whispered.

His hand moved down over the slight dome of her belly, and he felt her muscles jerk in involuntary response. He soothed her with slow, circular caresses, and after a while, his fingertips moved down again, into the soft thatch of curls at the base of her belly. Libby gasped.

Jake groaned aloud. He couldn't hold off much longer. One thing to be said for being forty—theoretically, at least—was the increased staying power. With Libby, even that slight advantage was shot all to hell. He felt like a randy teenaged stud, all raging hormones and no finesse.

"Libby," he whispered urgently, "sweetheart, I don't want to rush you, but—"

"Rush me! Please," she begged, grabbing his shoulders to pull him down to her.

Libby was stunned by her own aggressiveness. She had been accused of many things in her life. Aggressiveness was not among them. But did it matter in the long run who took the lead in something as inevitable as this? Beyond rational thought, she dug her fingers into the slippery skin of his shoulders and drew him closer.

Molten gold. Pure, hot molten gold flowed through her body as he parted the portals and entered. Libby gasped. Her eyes widened, and Jake buried his face in the curve of her throat.

"Don't—move," he grated. "Don't even breathe!"

She thought she might have moaned his name. She didn't breathe.

"It's been awhile for me, too," he said when he had himself under some sort of control.

For Libby it had been forever. Never in this lifetime had she experienced anything so utterly compelling, so utterly mind-shattering. So utterly, bone-meltingly *right!*

Driven beyond her meager limits, she lifted her hips and wrapped her legs around his waist. Jake's powerful body began to tremble.

"I wanted—for you, precious, I wanted it to be perfect," he gasped.

But it was already too late. Perfection was already upon them. Driven heedless, headlong into the flames together, they reached for the burning sun . . . and found it.

"So sweet," Jake breathed a long time later. "So very sweet."

It was the sound of the old furnace rumbling on that aroused him. Judging from the angle of the sun outside the window, little more than an hour had passed, but that was enough. It was too much, Jake thought ruefully as he pulled a lavender-scented comforter up over Libby's naked shoulder.

Jake, old man, you've really done it this time, he told himself as he quietly closed the bedroom door behind him. You thought one fast tumble and you'd be able to get her out of your system?

Man, you've lost it. This time, you really screwed up!

Naked, he stood in the kitchen and poured himself a cup of coffee. He took it straight, but it didn't help. Staring thoughtfully at the bedroom door down the hall, he wondered if he had the guts to sell out, move away and start all over again. Maybe somewhere in the Ozarks. Maybe California.

Hell, why not the moon, for all the good it would do? There were some things that distance couldn't cure. Might help. Time would help even more, but there were no real cures. That was another lesson he'd learned the hard way.

Passing her room in search of his clothes a few minutes later, Jake heard her moving around. The sound of dresser drawers opening and closing. On the way back to the kitchen he heard the sound of running water.

At least she took the time to get dressed before she came out to join him. If she'd come out of there in that damned bathrobe of hers—or worse yet, in nothing—he wouldn't have been responsible for his actions.

Jake had dressed in the utility room. His jeans were damp along the seams, his socks wet. He couldn't have cared less. The thing now was to get out of here before he did something irretrievably stupid.

Something *else* irretrievably stupid.

"Remember, we have to stop at the grocer's on the way back out to the cabin," Libby said, not quite meeting his eyes.

Jake's face turned to stone. Having forgotten completely that he was going to have to drive her back out there, he'd been mentally composing a tactful disappearance speech.

"Yeah, well...you want a cup of coffee to go? It's still hot."

He had downed three cups of the stuff. Other than eating a hole in his gut, the coffee hadn't done much for him. He hadn't experienced any blinding flashes of wisdom... although it was a bit late for wisdom now. Next time he'd try coffee first. Better yet, *instead* of.

But there wouldn't be any next time, he reminded himself. Not for Libby and him. She wasn't the first woman he'd slept with since Cass, not that there'd been that many. And none at all in a long time. Promiscuity had never been his style. Still, he had a feeling this one was going to take a lot more forgetting than any of the others had done. He had instinctively known that, right from the first.

So what the devil had happened to make him forget it? "Let's go then," he growled, covering uneasiness with anger. He didn't like the way she was looking at him.

And then he didn't like the way she was *not* looking at him. "Libby, it happened, okay? It's a little late to be having second thoughts, so why don't we both just agree to forget it?"

Jake felt, rather than saw, the impact his words had on her. Up went the chin, back went the shoulders. He cursed himself for being an insensitive son of a bitch. He called himself a coward and knew it for the truth.

The drive back out to the cabin was conducted almost as silently as the drive in had been. Libby ran into the Food Lion for cocoa, canned milk and marshmallows. She grabbed a package of Oreos and then tossed a couple of chocolate bars into her basket. David deserved a treat for losing his fish, she told herself, ignoring the fact that David's weakness was gingerbread, not chocolate. She was the chronic chocoholic in the family. Just let trouble rear its ugly head, and she dived for the comfort of a Hershey bar. This was going to be a three-bar night.

On arrival, Jake turned the truck around so that it was headed out before he switched off the engine. The message was hardly subtle. "It's getting pretty late," he said. "Guess I'd better run along."

"Yes, I expect so," she said with exquisite politeness, just as if the marks of her fingernails weren't still embossed on the skin of his buttocks.

Jake studied the persimmon tree a few feet away while Libby stole a glance at his rigid profile. Drawing a deep breath, she turned to stare out across the pond just as Jake turned to look at her.

"Jake, if you—"

"Yeah, I'd better get along," he said hurriedly, and blindly she opened her door. Jake was out before her feet hit the ground. "Libby," he began just as David dashed up and yanked on his mother's hand.

"Mama, Mama!"

Absently Libby rumpled her son's hair while her eyes met Jake's over the hood of his truck. "Thank you for the ride, Jake."

Oh, God, I didn't say that! Face flaming, she blundered on. "If you'd like to come back—well, I suppose you won't, but if you did—to fish, I mean—well, you're welcome."

Anytime, day or night, for the rest of my life, you're welcome.

"Mama, listen," David cried, hopping from one foot to the other.

Libby told herself that this was what she'd been unconsciously bracing herself against from the first time she'd laid eyes on him. She must have known instinctively that he wouldn't stay around much longer than it took to break her heart. "Yes, David, I'm listening, darling," she murmured absently.

She told herself she wasn't stupid. A slow learner, maybe, but not really stupid. No woman was proof against a man like Jake Hatcher. He had made it perfectly clear right from the first that he wasn't geared for double harness. What had happened didn't change that. Pushing away the sadness that threatened to engulf her, Libby told herself that Jake had his own problems. The last thing she needed was another man with problems. She had enough of her own.

"I'm listening, honey," she said, shifting her attention to her son. "Tell me while we take these things to Aunt Lula. I bought marshmallows for toasting, what do you think of that?"

But Jake wasn't quite finished yet. He came around the truck and stopped, so close he could see the gray strands woven among the gold in Libby's hair. David glared up at him, his belligerent features a smaller replica of his mother's in spite of his darker coloring. Jake squatted on his haunches until his eyes were level with the boy's. Gravely he said, "You want to take real good care of your mama, David. She had a bad scare today."

"My mama can swim," the child retorted. "She wouldn'a drownded even if you hadn'a pulled her out. I was going to jump in and save her!"

"I know you were. I just happened to be closer, that's all. When a woman needs help, we men have to do what needs doing, right?" His voice dropped to a lower note and came out sounding oddly husky. "She's lucky she has you, son. You're both luckier than you know."

For a long time afterward, Jake thought about the expression on the boy's face. David had looked as if the concept were one he had never heard of before, much less experienced firsthand. What a hell of a marriage she must have had.

Libby stood in the clearing and watched Jake's truck drive off down the winding, graveled road that connected her uncle's property with highway 158. Through the thicket of ancient field pines, she watched the glimmer of silver until it passed through the far gate, some quarter of a mile up the road, and disappeared from sight.

"Mama!" David tugged on her shirttail, and reluctantly she turned away. "Mama, I caught a three pounder! Uncle Calvin and me caught my rod and the fish was still on it, and Uncle Calvin said that was 'cause I hooked him real good. Jeffie caught two little ones, but I want to eat mine for supper. Please?"

Jake took two aspirins with water and stared at the bottle of Scotch. Somewhat to his surprise, he found that he wasn't particularly tempted. He'd lost count of the times in the past when he'd crawled into the bottle to escape the inescapable. No thanks to his own strength of character, he had eventually managed to crawl out again. And stay out. It was either that or die.

But whiskey wasn't going to solve anything now, any more than it had in the past. Not that he was ready yet to admit that there was anything to be solved.

Abruptly he turned back to the specs he had been staring at for the past hour or so and tried to focus on the figures there. It would be a first—a big first—if they decided to go after a chunk of the new interstate. Small and relatively new in the field, they'd be bidding against some of the biggest contractors in the region.

But Jake knew for a fact that some of the big firms were top heavy. Bostic had worked for one of their competitors for years before he'd gone into business for himself. Now the two of them ran a lean, mean outfit. Small profit margin, overhead cut to the bone, with every penny saved put into first-rate men and equipment. They were good at anticipating trouble. Even so, there were always surprises. Breakdowns. Illness. Freak weather conditions. It all had to be figured in.

It would be a challenge, and right now, Jake could do with something to occupy about a hundred and ten percent of his brain.

Was she still out there? Had she managed to stay dry? If she caught cold, was she going to blame it on him?

A wintry smile broke through the hard set of his features as he balanced the pencil between his two forefingers and stared out at an ugly brick warehouse across the street. He'd worked through about six inches of backlog so far. Only half a dozen more inches to go. If he hadn't played hooky this weekend, he'd have been caught up by now.

No, dammit, playing hooky described some schoolboy prank that might have got him grounded for a week or so. What he'd done was so supremely stupid he couldn't believe he had actually done it. It wasn't as if he hadn't known better, either. Right from the first she had got to him. A stranger across a crowded room—only in this case, the stranger had been married and extremely pregnant, and he had just seen Cass and Johnny and the baby-sitter off to the beach, and was already wondering what the devil he was doing still in town when they were somewhere else.

Libby Porter. He might have seen her in high school, he didn't remember. But he sure as hell remembered seeing her at the fund-raiser. Even then there had been something about her that had got to him. The next time he had seen her, at that reunion thing, he hadn't recognized her, not right off, but he had suspected even then she was a hazard. Like a bad allergy. Knowing he was susceptible, a smart man would have stayed the hell away.

So what did he do? He took her to bed. He sat around a camp fire with her friends and family, all cozy and warm and comfortable, and then he took her to bed!

Staring unseeingly at the bottle amid the scattered papers on his desk, Jake continued to argue with himself. What the hell, she was an experienced woman. She understood the rules of the game, didn't she?

But that was just it. She didn't. For all she'd been married and had a child, she was as green as they came. God, she didn't even know how to hide her feelings! It had been right there in her eyes, plain as day. She thought she was in love with him. What was infinitely worse, she had probably managed to convince herself, in spite of a total lack of encouragement on his part, that he was in love with her.

He wasn't. Anything he'd had to offer along those lines had been used up a long time ago. There was nothing left. He could live with that. He had lived with it for more than seven years. But she needed to know the score before she got in any deeper, because a woman's mind didn't work the way a man's did. Hell, Libby's mind didn't even work the way most women's did!

So okay. Just to be sure, he'd better let her know, in the kindest sort of way, that while he liked her and respected her, and enjoyed her company, maybe it would be best if—

Abruptly Jake threw down his pencil and glanced at his watch. It was late, but not all that late. The kids had probably flaked out by now, and the rest of the gang was probably sitting around the camp fire singing old cowboy songs.

Or maybe comparing notes on the joys of marriage, divorce and single parenthood.

Nine

This time instead of driving down and waking the camp, in case they were all asleep, Jake left his truck by the outer gate and cut through the woods on foot. He'd be lucky not to break a leg, he thought as he picked his way carefully through pines, hardwoods, brambles and muscadine vines.

From the edge of the clearing, he counted five people seated around the fire, which by now had burned down to no more than a rosy bed of coals. Even with her back to him, he had no trouble picking her out. Arms wrapped around her knees and head tilted in that characteristic way, she was listening to something the high school coach with the eight-year-old was saying.

Damned redneck jock! Jake knew the breed. Gullins was the type who considered any unattached female fair game. Babes, he called them. Broads. Sweet li'l ol' things whose sole purpose on earth was to keep his beer cold and his bed warm.

Jake started across the clearing, his powerful stride flattening the clumps of wild grass and pine seedlings that sprouted between infrequent mowings. That jackass had a few things to learn about Libby Porter! What's more, he'd better be a damn quick study, or Jake was going to clean his clock for him!

A woman's clear laughter rang out in the cold night air, and he froze. Libby's laughter? No—he'd have recognized her husky chuckle anywhere. This was the other woman, Jeffie's mom, Bunny what's-her-name.

Jeffie's mom. David's mom. Mickey's dad, Kyle's dad, Peanut's dad...

Slowly Jake's anger drained away, to be replaced by a bitter dose of reality. He had about as much business being here as a cat did in a goldfish bowl. Obviously this little shindig had been cooked up by Libby's aunt and uncle as an opportunity for her to meet men with whom she had at least one thing in common: single parenthood.

Oh, sure, they'd invited another woman along as a smoke screen. Calvin and Lula added additional cover. But their motive was unmistakable. The whole affair had been planned to give their niece an opportunity to look over the field without all the pressure attendant on the usual singles scene.

So where did Jake fit in? The answer was obvious. He didn't.

Feeling more an outsider than ever, Jake turned his back on the warm glow of shared laughter and shared interests. Far be it from him to spoil things for Libby. If she found fulfillment in toasting marshmallows around a camp fire with a bunch of PTA leftovers, far be it from him to cramp her style. God knows, he didn't have anything to offer her.

Libby decided that if Mike Gullins asked her out, she would go. Their children got along well enough together, although Mickey was something of a bully. It would probably do David good to get a taste of the real world. Having attended a small, excellent private academy for preschool, kindergarten and the first grade, he'd been sheltered, she admitted it freely. Since moving back she had often wondered if she was being unfair to him. Walt had accused her more than once of coddling the boy, but then Walt had consistently undermined her authority whenever she'd tried to be firm. She might never have had the nerve to end her marriage if she hadn't seen all too clearly what their constant tug-of-war was doing to David.

Just since yesterday, though, he had begun to accept the company of men. Nor did he seem particularly intimidated by the older kids, possibly because it was his uncle's pond, which gave him a certain stature. Not only had he had an opportunity to make new friends, he had learned that his mother could enjoy male friends of her own without threatening his security in any way. Nor did he seem as inclined, with several men to chose from, to latch on to any one of them the way he had that septic tank pumper-outer.

Oh, yes, the weekend had been a rousing success, Libby thought bitterly as she pretended to listen to a rundown on the care and feeding of a future football star. So why did she feel as if all the color had suddenly leached out of her world, leaving it in stark, lonely shades of gray?

By the middle of Sunday morning, the excitement had proved too much for the younger children. Jeffie had a stomach ache, Mickey had jerked a fishhook into his thumb and had to be driven to Mocksville to have it cut out. He had delighted the company afterward by telling them how it had swelled up and turned green when the doctor had stuck a needle in it and shot it full of gunk so it wouldn't hurt.

The little girl, Peanut, had settled into the whine mode, and Bunny was making a concerted effort to find out everything she could about Jake Hatcher.

"Hey, look, if I'm poaching on your preserves, just tell me to go jump," she said with engaging frankness. "But if you two don't have anything in particular going for you, I'd sure like to try my luck. It's got to be better than fishing!"

They both laughed, and Libby gave herself full credit for not yanking out those gorgeous, inch-long eyelashes. "You're welcome to try, as far as I'm concerned," she forced herself to say.

"So tell me everything. Where'd you meet him? How does he like his women—scrambled, fried, easy over?"

Unavailable, Libby could have said, but didn't. In small, strictly limited doses. "We went to high school together, but I really don't know all that much about him. He's single. He owns half a construction outfit. Not buildings—roads, bridges, that kind of thing. He dances, he doesn't drink, and he has an apartment somewhere north of town. I don't know the address, but he's probably in the phone book."

"You left out the most important parts, like he's got the face of a fallen angel and a body that can turn a perfectly sane woman into a raving maniac, but if you don't have sense enough to knock him down, tie him up and drag him off to your cave, then I'm going to give it my best shot. Wish me luck!"

Libby wished she'd walk into a tree and break her precious little turned-up nose in three places, but was too polite to say it.

They arrived home just after four. The sky had already turned a nasty shade of puce. Libby was low on groceries, she had a car full of muddy, fishy clothes, and a splitting headache. When David began to whine, first about not being able to go home with Jeffie, and then about going out for a hamburger, her patience snapped.

"First we are going to unload the car. Then we're going to clean up the fishing tackle and put it away. Then we're going to start a load of wash, and then we're going to go to the grocery store. And then maybe—maybe— we'll get supper while we're out."

David's yell of triumph made her wince, and Libby asked herself, not for the first time, if she was being too hard on him or too lenient. Could a mother ever make up for the absence of a father? How?

And all that was before she hurried into her bedroom to dump her overnight bag and saw the rumpled bed, with David's favorite quilt hanging over the back of her bent-willow rocking chair.

As if the rain weren't dismal enough, they both came down with colds the next day. Meet new kids, she thought philosophically, meet new germs. David's cold, as usual, settled in his ear, and Libby spent a small fortune on doctor's bills and antibiotics, expenses she had once taken for granted.

With the resilience of childhood, David recovered in three days. He was bursting with energy, and Libby saw him off on the bus every morning, counting down the

days before Walt was to pick him up for the following
weekend. *If* he didn't beg off at the last minute.

Evidently this time it was a go. When Walt called to
make arrangements to pick up David after school on Friday, he told her he had tickets to the State-Carolina game
on Saturday.

Libby wondered if he had the slightest conception of
how short a seven-year-old's attention span was. David
would survive it. Walt just might not.

Her own cold had settled in her chest. She could barely
talk. When Walt drove up and honked the horn on Friday afternoon, she was tempted to ignore him. Less than
an hour before, Jeffie had called and asked David over for
hot dogs, and he'd decided that would be more fun than
spending the weekend with his father.

"Daddy'll just yell at me a lot. He always yells at me,"
he'd said, and Libby had had her work cut out for her
changing his mind.

Not that she could blame him. Walt had never been
much of a father, but if he got the feeling that she was
trying to keep them apart, he could be extremely un-
pleasant.

"Hello, Walt. David's had a cold, and he's still on antibiotics. I've written instructions. Will you please see that
he takes his medicine every morning with his juice?"

Walt's habitually arrogant expression turned petulant.
"Oh, great. Just what I need, a sick kid."

"I'll be glad to let him stay home if you—"

"My mother's expecting him for dinner tonight."
Which explained a lot, Libby thought wryly. "You're
looking as beautiful as ever, Lib. Don't touch that, David. Are your hands clean? Libby, for God's sake, can't
you even keep him clean?"

"He just got home from school, but his hands are perfectly clean." As for her looks, Libby knew she looked awful. Colds always treated her this way. Her skin turned transparent, there were shadows a mile wide under each eye, and she had an even lower tolerance than usual for her ex-husband. "I'd appreciate it if you wouldn't keep him up too late."

"Give me credit for half a brain, will you?"

"Oh, I do, I do. I've always given you credit for half a brain."

Walt muttered something under his breath, making Libby feel about two inches high. She hadn't always been that way—petty and vindictive. Mean as a snake. It was the cold, she told herself. By the fourth day, she would have snapped at an alligator.

At least she had no worries about David's safety on the two-hour drive to Raleigh. Walt cared too much for his precious car to risk speeding. Besides, he'd already had more tickets than the law allowed. One more and he'd be lucky to be able to call a cab!

She was still feeling miserable, lonely and unattractive an hour later when the phone rang. Thinking it was Billy or Aunt Lula calling to inquire about her health, she croaked a greeting, and then, on hearing Jake's voice, was torn between hanging up and hanging on. By the time she came to her senses, he was begging her pardon for bothering her.

"Jake, it's not a wrong number, it's me!" she rasped. "Jake? Don't hang up."

"Libby, what the hell happened to your voice?"

"Oh, that. Our church choir's holding auditions for the Christmas Cantata. The soprano parts are all filled, but there's still an opening for a baritone." That was another thing about her and colds—three days on antihistamines and she got downright silly.

"You're crazy, lady, you know that? Certifiable."

"Tell me about it," she said morosely.

They were both silent for so long, Jake wondered if the connection had been broken. She couldn't regret what had happened any more than he did, but dammit, life went on. People made mistakes. The survivors picked up the pieces and went on from there.

Only Jake couldn't seem to move forward. "Look, I've got to be over in your neck of the woods later on this evening. We had a slight accident late yesterday with one of the dozers—this damned rain! Anyhow, I've had a crew out there all day, and I need to check by, so if you're going to be home, I thought I'd stop in. And say hello. To, ah—to David."

"Oh, well . . ."

"If you'd rather I didn't, all you have to do is say so."

She couldn't. She opened her mouth to tell him it would be better if he stayed away, but no sound emerged.

"About five, then. What if I stop by that barbecue place and bring along enough for half a dozen sandwiches?"

"Jake, you don't have to do that. David won't even be here!" As a protest, it was about as effective as an attack by a moth, her voice hitting on every third syllable. Jake ignored it. Now that he'd made up his mind to see her, he couldn't wait another minute.

He hung up the phone, stared down at his unsteady hand and wondered exactly when he had flipped out.

Libby didn't want him there. That's what she told herself as she raced through the house picking up toys, dishes, and straightening cushions and rugs. She repeated it while she showered, shampooed her hair and bent over from the waist to blow it dry with one hand while she polished her toenails with the other. Even half sick, she was efficient.

"Dammit, I didn't ask him to barge in here and mess up my life again," she muttered as she tried on one blouse after another, tossing them all onto the foot of the bed. "Just when I've got it together—just when—" She snatched off the peach flowered silk—for late November, yet!—and marched over to her dresser, where she dragged out her oldest sweatshirt. Once bright yellow, it had faded to the color of vanilla custard.

She sprayed a whiff of toilette water into the air and walked through it, then rushed to the bathroom and tried to scrub it off. He'd think she cared! He would probably think she had gone to great lengths to dress up for him.

Not if she could help it, he wouldn't, she told herself, and she had just started to strip off the custard-colored sweatshirt for a paint-spattered one when someone banged on the front door.

Muttering curses that came out as squeaks and wheezes, she strode to the door and flung it open. "Don't get close to me, I have a cold."

Her jaw was set on attack, and Jake resisted the urge to laugh. He resisted the urge to puncture her pitiful paper dragons, and he resisted, with far greater difficulty, the urge to drag her into his arms and kiss the living daylights out of her, cold germs, Olive Oyl voice and all.

"Here's this," he said instead, holding out a white paper sack.

"I told you David's not here."

His eyes gleamed briefly, and then he sauntered into the kitchen and placed the sack on the table. "I didn't want to take a chance on his coming home hungry. Besides, I can probably account for about three, myself."

"You ought to know better. Cholesterol."

Her arms were crossed over her breasts, her stance militant. Cheerfully Jake accepted the challenge. "I've never had a problem with the stuff. Good genes."

Before she could help herself, Libby's gaze dropped to the well-worn, close-fitting blue jeans. The way he was standing, with his legs crossed at the ankle and his hips braced against the kitchen table, he was blatantly, almost boastfully, male.

She had once heard an outspoken man described as an upfront kind of guy. Why the phrase should occur to her just now, she couldn't imagine.

Of course you can, you ninny, but it doesn't mean that!

"I've got all I need of the right kind, though," Jake went on. Libby closed her eyes as color swept up to her scalp. "HDL, LDL, LBJ—I never could keep up with these medical terms, but my doctor assures me that I've got the right mix of whatever's necessary. Blood pressure's fine, too, in case you were wondering."

Somehow, they got through the next few minutes. Libby explained about the custody agreement and the monthly visits, which as often as not ended up being canceled at the last minute, to no one's great disappointment. "Walt's taking him to a game tomorrow," she said with a slight frown. "I just hope it's not windy, because he has trouble with his ears."

"Does he have a hat?"

"Yes, but he won't wear it."

Somehow they got into a discussion of home remedies, and Libby soon forgot her concern over David's ears, which was probably what Jake had intended all along.

"Now, for a sore throat," he told her, "you can't beat a gargle of hot water, vinegar, black pepper and garlic. Works like a charm."

She shuddered. "No wonder you got out of pharmaceuticals."

Working together in surprising accord, they piled barbecue and slaw on buns, poured two glasses of milk and took the tray into the living room.

"Damper's still working all right, I see," Jake observed, testing the air for smoke.

"Thanks to you." Libby concentrated on not letting her sandwich fall apart in her hands. It looked wonderful. It tasted like rubber. At this rate, she might as well try his vinegar, pepper and garlic remedy. She wouldn't be able to taste it, and it might even help her voice. At least it didn't sound too fattening.

Sighing, she applied herself to her tasteless sandwich. That was another thing. Colds always made her feel fat.

Jake switched on her television set and tuned around to the news channel, giving them both something to stare at. Libby's eyes were too scratchy to wear contacts, but she refused to wear her glasses in front of Jake. On some women glasses were a fashion accessory. On Libby they were just glasses.

So she squinted. They sat side by side on the couch, not touching. Like two strangers in a bus station. The anchorman gloated over the bad news and cleverly put the usual negative spin on any good news that managed to squeeze in.

Libby gave up and concentrated on trying to decide whether or not the newscaster wore a hairpiece. He probably did. Shoulder pads, too. And didn't he used to have wattles?

Misery liked company. Feeling marginally better for having reduced a handsome, successful news anchor to a charlatan, Libby sighed and tucked her feet up beside her. Across the room in the ugly, old-fashioned fireplace, the logs burned hotly, sizzling occasionally as the flames found a hidden cache of sap.

Jake felt the tension that had ridden him all week begin to ebb, leaving him relaxed and oddly content. Had his parents ever spent an evening like this? If so, it was before his time. His grandparents, perhaps, at least in their early days, but by the time his parents had married, life for the Healys had already been complicated by too much money and too many commitments.

God knows, Cass would have thought he had lost his mind if he'd suggested a quiet evening at home together, sitting before the fire in companionable silence.

His gaze kept straying to the woman beside him. She looked tired. There were shadows under her eyes, and the tip of her nose was pink, which, oddly enough, only made her more attractive. It occurred to him that mid-life crises in the male of the species could be a very dicey proposition.

Jake knew he had no business being here. Yet here he was. Not only that, it felt right. They didn't have much in common, considering that they'd been classmates. Different backgrounds. Different upbringing. She had a child. He didn't. He played his cards pretty close to his vest, and Libby was an open book.

Yet in spite of all their differences, there was one thing they had in common, and that was a constant, deep-seated loneliness.

"Was that more rain?" Libby murmured, glancing at the window. With the clouds, it was already quite dark.

"Sounded more like sleet. It's early for that kind of weather."

"We've had snow in November before."

"If you really want to talk about the weather, Libby, we will. I'll talk about the nightly news, the stock market—whatever. But that's not what I came out here for."

Her stricken gaze flew to his, and Jake reached over and covered her hands. They were icy cold. "Quit it, now. I didn't mean what you're thinking."

"What was I thinking?"

"That I'd come out here to take you to bed again?"

"You'd never do that!"

The bleakness left his face, and he almost smiled. Drawing her against his side, he tucked her head into the hollow of his shoulder. "Listen, I've been doing some thinking."

"I'm almost afraid to ask," she murmured. She was shockingly aware of his chest under her cheek, the steady rhythm of his heart, the powerful arm around her shoulder, and the clean, masculine scent that eddied up from his warm body.

"Libby, I think we have something pretty valuable to offer each other. The thing is, we need to have an understanding."

"And you've just discovered this—this valuable thing we have? You didn't know about it last weekend?"

It was the antihistamine talking. Libby would never have asked a leading question like that. Just because a man and a woman slept together once, that didn't mean anything. An understanding, he'd said. Suddenly she wasn't at all sure she wanted to understand.

Jake's hand found its way under her hair, and he began stroking her nape, his fingertips rough on her sensitive skin. "No, I didn't just discover it. It's been there all along—I guess I just wasn't ready to admit it."

"What changed your mind?" She wasn't going to be taken in so easily, not again.

"I'm not really sure. A lot of little things begin to stand out in my mind. Gingerbread parts. Grocery carts. A certain attitude that's rare these days. I know, I know, it sounds crazy, but suddenly, things started to add up."

"I don't have the least idea what you're talking about. Jake, if this is a game, I told you, I'm not a very good player."

"It's no game, Libby. I'm not quite sure what it is, but I do know it's not a game."

She buried her face in his shoulder, her hands clenched in her lap. "That's what I'm afraid of. I think maybe games might be safer, after all."

For a long time, neither of them spoke. Freezing rain struck the window. A log shifted in the fireplace, and Libby thought about Rosa, who had helped raise David. She wished she'd remembered to ask Walt if the housekeeper would be there.

But of course, Walt would never have taken him without help. Mrs. Porter was good for the occasional lunch, but children made her nervous.

"Libby," Jake said, interrupting her vague concerns, "I never told you, but..."

She waited. After a while, he began to speak, and Libby held her breath, knowing intuitively that what he was going to say would somehow change her life.

"Seven years ago I had everything a man strives for. A beautiful wife, a—a son. A nice home, a successful business. Friends."

It was almost as if she'd known. As if his pain were her own.

"What happened?" she whispered.

And then in a voice devoid of emotion, in terms that could not possibly be misunderstood, he began to tell her.

Ten

Sometime during the telling, the sleet had turned to rain. The fire had burned down to glowing coals, and for a while, neither of them spoke. Then, Libby covered Jake's hand with her own and she squeezed. Hard.

"Sorry for dumping on you that way," he said, his voice sounding uncomfortably raw.

"Jake, don't." Pressing her face into the hollow of his shoulder, she held him tightly around the waist. This, then, was the cause of that deep well of sadness she had sensed in him right from the first. To lose a child, a bright, beloved son—to have him one moment and lose him forever in the next, would be pain beyond bearing.

"There aren't any words," she whispered. "There just aren't." He hadn't said all that much about his wife, but he had to have loved her. Libby would have given all she possessed to be the woman Jake loved. To have the right to share his grief, to share his life. To give him another child, even though it could never take the place of the one lost.

Abruptly Jake leaned his head back. His eyes felt as if they were bleeding. He felt raw all over, yet oddly light, as if he'd shed a great weight.

In a sense, perhaps he had. The first few days after it had happened, he had sealed himself off. In shock, he had moved through whole blocks of time like a sleepwalker, making all the arrangements, saying all the right things to the right people. Dealing with Cass, who had been dealing with her own burden of guilt and pain. By convincing himself that he was handling it, he had managed to avoid facing up to reality. A month passed, and then a year. By the time the enormity of his loss finally caught up with him, he was completely alone.

He'd told Bostic a pared-down version of the truth. That he had lost a son and a wife, sold what was left of his business before he could lose that, too, tried to drown himself in booze, landed in jail on a D-and-D charge, and finally figured if he was going to kill himself, a bullet would be a hell of a lot simpler all around.

The old man hadn't asked for details. Jake hadn't offered any.

Now he thanked God for Libby's arms. She hadn't offered him sympathy—not in empty words. Nor had she asked any questions. After a while she shifted into a more comfortable position, and then was still so long he wondered if she'd fallen asleep.

"I was almost glad David was going to spend this weekend with Walt, even though he didn't want to go. He never does," she added apologetically. "But we've both been short-tempered this past week, and I thought it would do us both good to be apart for a weekend. Now I wish he hadn't gone."

"Don't. Honey, don't, for God's sake, feel guilty just because you're a human being. I've been down that road, and believe me, it doesn't go anywhere."

"I tried to tell myself it was because those two need each other, but that's not true. Walt was always buying him these expensive toys. You know, radio-operated model airplanes and an ATV when he wasn't even big enough to ride a bike. And then he'd get mad because David didn't know how to use them properly, and they'd get put away. David would cry and Walt would blame me for the whole debacle."

Jake pinched the space between his brows. "My father gave me his father's set of lead soldiers. That was just about the time they discovered that lead wasn't among the preferred food groups. My mother pitched a fit, and I never got to play with the things. I didn't bother to offer them to Johnny."

They talked, of all things, about favorite toys—Johnny's books and pirate hat. David's construction set and soldier doll. Jake's favorite had been a wooden logging truck. Libby's, a homemade stuffed monkey.

"A stuffed monkey? I thought all little girls liked dolls. Cass still had Ken and Barbie and trunks full of clothes when we were married."

"Oscar was so skinny—the stuffing in his tail was so lumpy, I had to adopt him because I knew no one else ever would. He was so ugly, I crocheted him this hideous sweater out of pink rug yarn, but that didn't help much, I'm afraid."

Jake nodded understandingly. They fell into a benign silence—a healing silence. When Libby offered to make coffee, he was glad for an excuse to escape the compelling ambience of the comfortably shabby parlor, with the comfortably worn furnishings. There was such a thing as being *too* comfortable.

"It's late," he said while the coffee was dripping. "I ought to be leaving pretty soon."

"Stay and have your coffee first. Maybe by then it'll have stopped raining."

Libby wasn't all that interested in coffee. She suspected Jake wasn't, either. She simply hated the thought of his being alone on a cold, rainy night. For all his outward strength, she had a feeling that deep down inside, he was even more vulnerable than she was.

Not that you would ever know it to look at him, leaning against the counter with his legs crossed at the ankles and thumbs hooked under his belt loops, with that padlocked look on his face.

Libby took a deep breath. Then, before she could lose her nerve, she said, "Jake, stay here tonight."

Jake's eyebrows plunged like a pair of diving hawks, and like a helpless rabbit, Libby waited for the feel of his talons in her back. She'd always been a social disaster, but this surpassed even her record. "I didn't mean—"

"Libby, you don't have to—"

"No, listen to me." Her mangled attempt at an explanation only made things worse. "I'm not asking for anything, Jake—not for myself. I just can't bear to think of your driving across town alone on a night like this, to an empty apartment. That is, it might not be empty. I mean, you probably have lots of—um . . ." Her unreliable voice wavered off, making her wish her vocal chords had given out before her brain had. "What I meant was that since David isn't here, you're welcome to use his room. Oh, lord, I'm sorry," she finished helplessly. It wasn't bad enough to make a fool of herself, she had to do it in a voice like a rusty hinge! "Oh, crud," she muttered, utterly defeated.

"Don't apologize. If you mean it, I'd like to stay, but Libby—if I stay, it won't be in David's room. You understand?"

She nodded. It was what she'd truly intended, after all, and not on account of the rain. At least not altogether.

Jake poured coffee into two mugs and Libby turned out the lights and locked up. He didn't have pajamas, and she didn't have anything that would come near fitting him.

"I have germs," she reminded him.

He placed the two mugs on the bedside table and began unbuttoning his shirt. "Nothing I can't handle."

"I hope you won't be sorry." And trying desperately for lightness, she added, "I can always heat you some pickle juice if your throat starts getting sore."

"And I'll massage your chest for you. It sounds pretty congested."

Her eyes, shadows notwithstanding, glinted with laughter. "You're too generous. Shall I mix up a mustard plaster?"

"Do and you'll sleep alone," Jake teased.

"So that's the secret of turning aside unwanted masculine attention. Not that I ever had all that much trouble."

"The men must have been blind."

Libby stepped into the bathroom. Through the thin paneled door she could hear Jake moving around in her bedroom. She still couldn't believe she had asked a man to spend the night with her.

Yet, how could she have let him go after what he had told her tonight? He needed her, she told herself. And she needed whatever she could have of him—whatever was left over from Johnny and Cass, even if it wasn't exactly love.

The sheets were cold; Libby usually wore socks to bed in the wintertime, but somehow, it didn't seem fitting under the circumstances.

"Aren't you freezing?" she asked as they sat and sipped their coffee, leaning against the headboard.

"No. Are you?"

"My feet are. My clock runs down when I have a cold."

"I could wind it for you." Jake's offer was accompanied by something resembling a tired leer.

But they both knew it was too soon. Here she was, Libby thought, in bed with the most beautiful man God had ever put together, and all she wanted to do was hold him. It had to be her cold. How could any woman feel sexy knowing she sounded like a bullfrog and probably looked even worse?

Beside her, Jake thought of all the places he could have been tonight. At that country-western bar with the cute little radiologist who'd called him just last week. He had dated her a few times last summer. Or with Gillie, drinking seltzer over near the School of the Arts, listening to some Irish dudes playing drums and pennywhistles.

The last place he had expected to find himself was here in Libby's bed, yet he could think of nowhere he'd rather be. And oddly enough, not for the usual reason—although he wasn't fool enough to believe that condition would last much longer.

Jake placed his cup on the table and switched out the light. Libby wiggled down under the covers and waited to see what came next. Whatever he needed from her tonight was his for the asking. Tonight and always.

With no conscious thought, they spooned together, Libby on her left side, Jake curved around her. She placed the soles of her feet on his shins, and his arm around her waist tightened convulsively. "You weren't kidding about cold feet, were you, honey?"

"I warned you."

"Next time, wear socks."

"I usually do, but I was afraid you'd laugh."

"Never," he vowed. She could feel him shaking, but he didn't utter a sound. His breath caressed her cheek and his hand spread over her stomach, sending a coil of warmth deep inside her, where she had been cold for too long. "I'm not laughing, honey, honest."

"Just wait until you come down with my cold, then we'll see who laughs last."

"Quit threatening me and go to sleep, will you?" He chuckled, and Libby closed her eyes and smiled into her pillow.

Libby never knew what had awakened her. A branch striking the side of the house? The wheezing old mantel clock in the living room that struck only when it took a notion to?

Jake had been awake for several minutes. He had woken up with his usual morning erection, and was trying to convince himself that a cold shower would be a hell of a lot safer, all things considered.

"Did you say something?" Libby murmured sleepily.

"Uh-uh. Go back to sleep, honey."

"Mmm, it's so nice and warm." She snuggled her plump backside into his pelvic region, and he groaned.

Warm. Right. Try hot as a firecracker. With a short fuse.

He knew the minute she felt him. She stiffened, trying to pretend she hadn't noticed anything out of the ordinary.

"Nothing personal," he said gruffly, and then wondered if she was fool enough to believe him. Hell yes, it was personal! As a largely celibate male, it was nothing he wasn't used to dealing with. Any other morning, he might have swung out of bed, done a few calisthenics, hit the shower and been right as rain by the time he had his eyes open good.

Only this wasn't any other morning. This was the morning after he'd spilled his guts for the first time since Johnny had died. This was the morning after he had shared a bed with a woman, asking nothing of her but the comfort of holding and being held.

This wasn't any other morning, and this wasn't any other woman. This was Libby. Jake turned her face toward him and kissed the corner of her mouth. It was going to take more than a few morning exercises and a long cold shower to cure what ailed him this time.

"Libby?" he asked tentatively, and when she rolled over and buried her face in his throat, he swallowed hard and crushed her against him. *Libby, Libby, what are you doing to me? What am I going to do about you?*

Libby had already given her heart, unconditionally. For all the good it had done to tell herself it wasn't wise, wasn't even wanted, she had done it anyway. Now she offered her body with the same reckless generosity.

Jake managed to regain control of his emotions, but his hands were none too steady as he lifted the cotton night-gown over her head. Not one word had she spoken, but it was there in her eyes, the same way it had been before. More than he was ready to see. More than he was ready to accept.

"Honey, if you don't want—"

She covered his mouth with her fingertips. "I want," she said simply, and it was all the encouragement he needed. Later on he might have regrets. Later on he might reconsider the wisdom of letting himself get this involved, but right now he was beyond the reach of reason.

Her body was deliciously warm. She smelled faintly of soap, faintly of woman, and Jake knelt above her and let his hands follow his gaze down her body, over her smooth shoulders, over the small, full breasts with their dusky rose nipples.

He lowered his face to her breasts, savoring the warmth, rubbing the hardened tips with his beard-roughened cheek before bathing them with his tongue. Libby whimpered, moving restlessly under his attentions. Gray morning light spilled in through the window, highlighting the pewter threads in his hair, and she pressed his head tightly against her breast.

But Jake was not a man to be held for long. He explored with equal thoroughness every soft inch of her trembling body, claiming with lingering kisses the dimples behind her knees, the hollows behind her ankles, the soft swell of her belly and more.

Ah, much, much more...

When neither of them could stand to wait a moment longer, he positioned himself and lifted her hips onto his own thighs. Then he drew her up until the pouting tips of her breasts brushed against his chest, lifted her again, and brought her down on him, slowly, slowly, drawing out the exquisite pleasure until they were both nearly out of their minds.

"My God, woman, what have you done to me?" he groaned.

Libby was beyond speech. She wrapped her arms around him and clung even as her body joined his in a dance as compelling as time itself.

Jake hung on to his own control until he felt her seizures commence. And then, as her tight, hot sheath began to convulse around him, hurtling him toward his own climax, he shouted aloud.

A long time later they lay together, still entwined, with covers tangled around them. Jake felt the cold air on his back, but his front was burning, melded as tightly as possible to the heat of Libby's body. He stared blindly at the pale, striped wallpaper, at the corner of a wicker-framed mirror.

What was happening to him? What was this thing that had taken root in him when he wasn't looking? Carnal needs he could understand, but this went far beyond anything he had ever experienced before. Was it because he had confided in her? Was it because she had a son?

But that was crazy! He and the kid didn't even like each other. If anything, David was a complication.

Carefully he put her away from him and rolled over onto his back, staring up at the stained ceiling. Her roof had a leak, he thought absently. He wondered if she'd had it patched yet. Hell, it was only good sex. All right, great sex. But that's all it was, all he was looking for. He wasn't in the market for anything else. He had let her know how he felt about that right up front.

Hadn't he?

Libby felt a draft of cold air where there was none to be felt. She drew the covers up under her chin and wished it was still dark, so she could make a dash for the bathroom. She needed to shower and dress so she could think straight.

Although it was a little late now for thinking. If she had been in any doubt as to her feelings before, she could no longer deny the truth. After last night she could no longer hope to get over it, no longer pretend that it was only a woman's normal reaction to an attractive, likable man. The plain truth was that what she felt for Jake Hatcher was deeper, wider, richer by far than anything she had ever felt before. She wanted to be his lover, his friend, the mother of his children. The keeper of his dreams.

In other words, she thought ruefully, the same old syndrome. She wanted to give far more than anyone wanted to receive.

"Do you want the bathroom first?" she made herself ask.

"You go first. I'd better make a few calls, see if everything's all right on the site."

"You work on weekends?" she asked, forcing a bright look of interest.

Jake reached for his watch and strapped it on, not meeting her eyes. "With a dozer in a ditch, you work the clock around and then some. Reckon there's any coffee left over from last night?"

But before either of them could get out of bed, the phone rang. Libby grabbed her nightgown and hauled it over her head, wrong side out, and raced out to the hall.

"You ought to have a jack installed in your—" The words cut off abruptly. After one look at her stricken face, Jake was out of bed like a shot, stark naked. Standing behind her, he rasped, "Libby, what is it? What's wrong?"

"It's David," she said slowly. "He's disappeared!"

Jake took over. While Libby showered and dressed, he checked the levels in his car, placed a few calls and then burned several slices of toast. While she forced down a single slice, he showered and dressed, not taking time to shave.

"We'll take my car," he said tersely, helping her into her raincoat.

"Jake, that's not necessary. It's a two-hour drive. I know Walt's doing everything that can possibly be done. David can't have gone far." She had to believe that, or she'd die!

Jake could tell how much her tenuous control was costing her. He didn't bother to reply, but herded her outside and into the passenger seat of his own car. "At least I have a phone. You won't have to wait for two hours to find out what's going on."

She looked as brittle as glass, her eyes too large, too wild. Dear God, he thought, in silent supplication, let it be all right. Don't let it happen again, not this time!

Libby gave him Walt's number, and once out of city traffic, Jake placed the call and handed Libby the phone. "Who are you?" she asked. And then, "Oh. Have you heard anything, anything at all? Has Walt called the police? What about the—yes, I know, but—"

There was more. Jake waited, his mind clicking over rapidly, and then he took the phone from her. "Libby? What's happened?" His second thought had been a ransom kidnapping. Porter would be a likely target.

His first thought he had forcefully put out of his mind. He'd give anything if he hadn't told Libby about Johnny. It would be fresh on her mind, a reminder she didn't need of a worst-case scenario. "Libby?" he prodded when she sat there, frozen, staring straight ahead.

"A friend of Walt's answered." Her voice was unnaturally calm. "She said her name was Denise. Walt's not there. She's taking messages."

"And?" Jake prompted when she fell silent again.

"And? Oh... They don't know anything else. The three of them went to the game yesterday, and David wasn't feeling good by the time they got home, so he went to bed. Rosa sat with him." Rosa. Jake figured her for a baby-sitter, and didn't interrupt. Libby needed to talk, not to seal herself off. "Denise said as far as she knew, he was just fine last night when she and Walt got home, but when he didn't come down to breakfast, Walt sent Rosa upstairs after him and he was..." She swallowed hard, her hands knotted tightly in her lap. Reaching over, Jake took her left one and spread it over his thigh, holding it there.

"What about his clothes?"

"His clothes?" She sounded dazed. "I don't know."

"You said he didn't feel good. Is there any chance he might have got up in the night to—you know—throw up or something—and wandered back into the wrong room by mistake?"

"He has his own bathroom right off his old room."

She lapsed into silence again, and Jake concentrated on getting through traffic. It was heavy, and the rain had started up again. He considered turning on the radio and decided against it. Music wouldn't help, much less the usual body count that passed for local news these days. Jake pulled in at the rest stop and made her get out and walk around for a few minutes, rain or no rain. She needed a break. No, dammit, she needed to bend *before* she broke!

While she was in the bathroom, he raided the machines. She needed fuel. One piece of burned toast wasn't going to get her through the next few hours.

He had never seen the Porter place, but the neighborhood was pretty much what he'd expected. Wooded lots, about ten acres and up. A few rock and glass, but mostly old brick or new brick whitewashed to look old. Pricy landscaping, glassed-in swimming pools, tennis courts—

the usual. It was a far cry from this place to the house where Libby lived now.

He wondered why. He wondered a lot of things that were none of his business, but that could wait.

Porter was there when they drove up. There were half a dozen cars in the paved circular drive, most with the carefully anonymous look that screamed police. With Porter's clout, the FBI had probably already been called in if there was the slightest hint that the boy had been snatched.

A uniformed woman, stick-thin, with black eyes and gingery hair, started bawling the minute they stepped inside. She embraced Libby with a stranglehold, and then stepped back, wiped her red-rimmed eyes and offered them both coffee and homemade buns. "I'm just so sorry, I can't tell you! I sat with David myself last night. I read to him until he went off to sleep. I declare, I thought he was all right! He said his stomach was a-botherin' him early on, but he didn't have a fever."

"I know, I know. It's not your fault, Rosa. But didn't anyone hear anything?"

"Not that I know of. I sat in the kitchen and watched the TV until Mr. Porter and Miss Keith came in, and then I went to bed. First thing I knew was when Mr. Porter called me this morning. I'm so sorry, I just don't know what to do! That poor little baby!"

Jake stood apart, watching while Porter conferred with one group of men and then another. The bimbo in tights and a big gauzy tent shirt perched on the arm of a chair and tried to look concerned, but as she kept glancing at her reflection in the glass patio doors and rearranging her pose, Jake didn't find the act particularly convincing.

God help the boy if this was his stepmother.

When the housekeeper began crying on Libby's shoulder again, Jake moved in to the rescue. Drawing Libby off to one side, he said, "I'm sure the house has been turned upside down, but what about the grounds? What about any playmates he might have in the neighborhood?"

Libby pulled herself together. Disregarding her exhusband, who seemed to be doing little more than throwing his weight around and generally making an ass of himself, she turned to a man in a glen plaid suit. He had a look of authority about him, as well as a look of distaste for Walter Bettinger Porter III.

"Would you please tell me everything? I'm David's mother."

The officer took her into another room, and Jake started after them, then stopped. He was an outsider. He had no rights at all. He was there only as Libby's friend—as something more than a friend, he admitted silently. Something a hell of a lot more.

But that would have to wait.

Eleven

From the elegant Danish leather chair, Jake watched her closely. They had been there less than an hour, and since the first few minutes after their arrival he had been battling a powerful urge to get her the hell out of there.

And take her where?

God knows. At least to someplace where he stood a chance of protecting her. This was Porter's territory. It might have been Libby's home once, but somehow Porter had ended up keeping it while his wife and son had been relegated to a dump in the country some hundred miles away. Prenuptial agreement? Old family property? Total lack of integrity?

Stroking his itchy jaw, Jake wondered what she had seen in the man. There must have been something between them, but for the life of him, Jake couldn't figure it. Libby had more class in her little finger than that pedigreed blowhard would ever have.

On the other hand, she had married him. They'd had a child together. And no matter how protective Jake was feeling, he'd better keep in mind the fact that he was here on sufferance.

With a feeling of impotence, he watched as she moved restlessly around the room, touching a chair here, a table there. He tried to picture her in that setting, and failed. When she paused to stare out through an expanse of glass at the carefully naturalized grounds, he ached to go stand behind her, beside her.

But sympathy wasn't what she needed now. She was going to have to find within herself whatever strength it took to sustain her, because regardless of the outcome, Jake had a feeling Porter was going to be no help at all. If the boy was—

He swore silently. Neither all the king's horses nor all the king's men would be able to help her if the worst happened. All he could do was bleed for her. And pray—not that he had much clout in that particular arena.

Come on, Libby love, hang in there. It's not going to happen this time. Not again, please God.

She seemed to grow taller. Backlit from the tall window, her hair gleaming like a silvery halo, she squared her shoulders and lifted her head in a familiar gesture, and Jake felt something deep inside him crumble and wash away in a warm, healing tide.

He just hoped to hell that attitude of hers would get her through the next few hours. After that…well, they'd just have to take it one step at a time. Whatever happened, he would be there for her.

Unobtrusively Jake continued to watch the shifting tableau from across the room. He knew he must look like hell, wearing yesterday's rumpled clothes. His unshaved jaw was itching for a razor, and he felt a fierce desire for a cigarette.

So far, no one had challenged his right to be here, although Porter had sent him several suspicious looks. Under the circumstances, he couldn't much blame the poor bastard.

Libby pulled herself together. She took a deep, steadying breath, not daring to look at Jake for fear she would hurl herself into his arms and start crying. Crying wasn't going to help. With her congestion, she would probably asphyxiate herself!

Instead she turned to where Rosa hovered in the dining-room door, wringing her hands. The housekeeper was blaming herself. Libby knew that Rosa couldn't have loved David more if he'd been her own child. She would have moved to Winston-Salem with them if Libby could have afforded to keep her.

"My poor baby," the older woman cried softly, and Libby slid an arm around her narrow waist.

"Rosa, he's probably just hiding somewhere. You know David—he's as independent as a hog on ice. Always has been." But not since the separation. Not since his whole life had been turned upside down.

With quiet authority, Libby instructed the woman to make sandwiches and another pot of coffee and set them out on the buffet. That done, she turned to Walt and the policeman, who was asking about David's state of mind when last seen.

Libby shuddered at the term "when last seen." It sounded horribly like something one might hear on the six o'clock news, and she refused to think about David that way.

"He was fine," Porter said with a shrug. "Like I said earlier, we went to the game—I always have seats on the fifty-yard line. After the game, we drove directly to the club. We usually have dinner there on weekends. He'd gotten sort of whiny during the last half—you know how kids are. Wanting this, wanting that, needing to go to the bathroom every five minutes.''

From across the room, Jake listened, picturing the scene easily. The jerk should have known better than to drag a seven-year-old kid through that mob. Whatever happened to Saturday afternoons at the zoo, with ice-cream cones and peanuts?

"The real trouble started," Porter went on, "when he pitched a fit over that damned rag doll my esteemed ex-wife lets him drag around.'' He shot her a scathing glance that made Jake's fingers ache to throttle him.

"You say he pitched a fit. You wanna describe that? Did he cry? Did he complain? Did he lose the doll or something?''

"No, he didn't lose the doll or something," Walt sneered. "I wish to God he had! I didn't notice the thing when we left home because he sneaked it out in his coat. I made him leave it in the car during the game, and that started it. When we got to the club, I told him to leave the thing in the car—they have an excellent nursery there. There was no need to drag in a piece of garbage that came from God knows where! Anyway, David refused to get out of the car, and one thing led to another. You know how it goes.''

"Miss Keith," the officer began, but Porter interrupted before she could speak.

"Denise can tell you. We had plans to meet friends for dinner and needless to say, we were nearly an hour late. Denise tried to reason with the little wretch, but we finally had to give in and bring him home.''

"You stayed here after that, then?''

Walt shrugged his shoulders dismissively. "Rosa was here. I told you we had an engagement. We dropped David off and went back to salvage what we could of the evening."

The officer had taken out a notebook and was jotting something down. He looked up and said, "This—uh, tantrum? Could you describe it? About how long did it last? What was the boy's state of mind when it was over?"

"Kicking, screaming, crying—for God's sake, haven't you ever seen a child have a tantrum before? I assure you, David has it down to a fine art by now. We both tried to reason with him. Miss Keith went out of her way to be friendly, but it seems my son has developed a few discipline problems while living with his mother." He shot Libby a malicious look. "I had to force him to apologize to her more than once, I can tell you."

Eyes narrowed, Jake was watching Libby. Her back was ramrod straight, that jaw of hers so square it could have chipped flint. She was ready to blow, and Jake couldn't blame her. The bastard didn't even have sense enough to know what a bastard he was!

Quietly Jake moved closer, ready to pick up the pieces if need be. In the back of his mind, a picture was beginning to form. Certain elements were beginning to come together....

Curiously Jake studied Porter's girlfriend. He didn't think she was the same one who'd been crawling all over him that night seven years ago, when Libby had got sick of the whole rotten scene and left. Cast from the same mold, though. Pretty enough in a vapid sort of way. Probably good-natured, but not too bright. Although she was evidently bright enough to have earned herself a pair of diamond dangle earrings that weighed in at about three carats each.

Damn Porter, Jake cursed silently. He could at least have had the decency to get his playmate out of sight! Although Libby was taking it like a thoroughbred. Not so much as a raised eyebrow at the introduction. It must have galled the hell out of Porter to find himself outclassed by the daughter of a small-time farmer. Jake had an idea that Porter's ego was founded more on the proceeds from a long line of robber barons than on any real accomplishments of his own. It was a risk among the silver-spoon set. After a few generations, the stock had a tendency to run to seed.

Libby tugged at Porter's sleeve, and Jake's hands unconsciously knotted into fists. "Walt, did David say anything yesterday about visiting any of his old playmates? He might have wanted to go play with the Walser boys, or even Peggy Lee Boren. Do the Borens still live on the corner? Have you called?"

Porter sent her a withering look. "Why don't you just go somewhere and have a nice quiet breakdown? I'm handling this, Libby!"

"Yes, but—" She stammered, and he deliberately turned his back on her.

Jake took her arm. "Libby, come into the kitchen where we can talk," he said quietly.

Walt spun around again, his even features marred by a sullen cast. "Just who the hell are you, anyway?" he demanded. "This is a family matter, so why don't you just butt the hell out!"

At a superficial glance, the two men were somewhat alike. Both were tall, both were dark, both had that indefinable air that hinted at a certain type of background. A closer look revealed that Walt's polish was only a surface patina, covering weakness and a lack of self-discipline, whereas Jake's was bone-deep, undiminished by rumpled clothing or an unshaved jaw.

Libby took hold of Jake's arm and urged him toward the kitchen. It was like trying to drag a bulldog away from a spitting cat. "Jake, let's go."

"Yeah, why don't you do that?" Porter snarled. "Obviously my ex-wife's taste in boyfriends is having a lousy influence on my son. Maybe I'll have my lawyer look into the custody thing again."

Which was so patently unfair under the circumstances that even Porter had the grace to look embarrassed. As far as Jake was concerned, that was all that saved him. That and the fact that regardless of the satisfaction to be gained from driving the bastard's nose through the back of his skull, Libby would be the one to suffer for it.

Every eye in the room was focused on the two men. The policeman's gray eyes were cool and speculative, the housekeeper's brown ones worried, Denise Keith's, underneath layers of navy mascara and frosted blue eyeshadow, openly curious.

But it was Libby's green eyes, haunted and unnaturally calm, that really got to him. Wrapping his arm around her, Jake drew her across the room, leaving Porter staring after them.

"Breathe, honey," Jake murmured. "Take a deep breath...that's right. Now do it again. You know he's only rattling his sword. He's scared, too. Give him credit for that much."

"Only if I have to."

Jake's smile didn't quite reach his eyes. "Right. The poor jerk has to feel guilty as sin on account of David disappearing on his watch. I reckon he's dealing with it the only way he knows how."

Libby breathed deeply in and out a few more times, and Jake wondered briefly if he should warn her against hyperventilation. "I've been thinking," he said. "Let me run something by you, okay? You remember telling me how David reacted whenever he thought you might be getting interested in a man?"

Libby looked puzzled. Rosa hovered over them, forcing on them food that neither of them wanted while Jake outlined his theory. Ignoring the chicken salad sandwich set before her, Libby heard him out.

When he was finished, she gripped the edge of the table until her knuckles showed white. "Jake, if you're right, then he might just be hiding! But wouldn't the policeman have thought of that?"

"The guy's not married. He obviously hasn't the least idea about how a kid that age might react to the notion of a new stepmother. Or stepfather, for that matter. In a case like this, any cop would probably be inclined to think of a ransom kidnapping, if not a custody snatch." He covered her hand with his. "Libby, I don't want you to get your hopes up too high, but I'd say there's an outside chance that Miss Keith might've given David the impression, deliberately or otherwise, that she and Porter will be getting married. You'd know better than anyone else how he would react to that."

"But he already has me. He doesn't need another mother."

"I know. And neither Porter nor his girlfriend strikes me as the nurturing type. Still, you never know how a kid's mind works. I overheard a few of the boys at your uncle's place comparing notes. David's little friend Petey told some pretty bloodcurdling tales about his stepmother. Kid's got a great future as the next Stephen King."

"I'd never thought about... But it makes sense. Remember my telling you how he is with men? Either he hates them on sight or he wants me to marry them?"

"Somehow, I don't think he took to Miss Keith."

"He threatened to blow up the plumber, but there was this septic-tank man right after we moved back home—he had a new tank wagon, with dual wheels and lots of hoses and gears and things, and David decided he'd make a dandy new father."

"Remind me to show him our new John Deere 892," Jake muttered. And then, giving her hand a squeeze and releasing it, he said, "Okay, honey, you find a phone and start calling around. Everything you say will probably be taped, but that's no problem. Just call all the places you can think of, even those that aren't all that close. Neighbors, playmates—everyone. Describe what he was wearing and find out if anyone's seen him since yesterday."

The cops would have already done all that, but something—just an insignificant detail—might have slipped their minds the first time. More important, Libby needed something to focus on. There was a brittle look about her that worried him. "What was he wearing?"

"His green coat, yellow sneakers—jeans, of course. And Ikky."

"Ikky," Jake repeated. "I'm afraid to ask."

She smiled, and it was like the sun coming out after a forty-day rain. "You know. Ikky. David's best friend, but don't make the mistake of calling it a rag doll. Boys don't play with dolls."

"Right. The Gulf War hero."

"Church bazaar edition. Homemade camouflage fatigues and yellow yarn hair. You'll recognize him if you see him, because David will be physically attached to the thing."

"Right." Shoving back his chair, Jake got to his feet. "You go get started calling around while I scout the grounds. I know they've been thoroughly searched, but little boys can hide in surprisingly small spaces. Kinda like mice." He was trying for another smile, but he guessed that was too much to hope for. "Meet you back here in—" he glanced at his watch "—an hour. Either way."

And then, gently he reached up and cupped her chin, lifting it until her eyes met his. "Attitude, honey," he said softly. "We're going to win this one, I promise you."

Somehow, someway, God, we've got to win this one!

Forty-five minutes later, Jake wasn't so sure. He'd given the place a cursory once-over on the way in. At first glance, it had seemed like a boy's paradise, full of trees, with a greenhouse, a stable, a three-car, two-story garage. Hundreds of potential hiding places.

The greenhouse had been easy. It was empty. Evidently Libby had been the horticulturist, not Porter. There was a handsome chestnut gelding in the stable. Jake was no expert, but he'd bet even money the horse had cost more than his own car had. He searched the empty stalls, the loft and the tack room and then headed for the garage.

On the way, he scanned the terrain. The underbrush had been carefully controlled, kept mainly to rhododendrons and ferns that looked wild, but probably weren't. There was an artfully arranged clump of rocks at one end of what appeared to be a dry creek bed.

On an impulse, Jake turned in that direction. There was no water, thank God, not even a trickle, in spite of the recent rain. But evidently the thing flooded occasionally, because there was a culvert under the driveway, half-hidden now by dead leaves.

A culvert... Now why did that ring a bell?

It was midafternoon. The weather was cold and unsettled. It might not freeze tonight, but it would be too damned cold for a kid to be sleeping out.

Davie, come on, boy—where are are you?

A few leaves fluttered down from the gums, oaks and sycamores. Jake stood still, the damp wind cutting through his lightweight jacket, while he studied the lacy network of branches overhead. Where would a boy go to hide when the going got rough? Where would he hole up to keep the real world at bay? A playhouse?

No. Libby would have mentioned a playhouse.

Johnny, help me on this one, will you, son?

The creek bed drew his gaze again. Unbidden, he pictured a sudden rush of muddy brown water breaking through a dam of debris, following a timeworn course through the hilly country. He pictured a small boy kneeling in the dry bed, playing with his toy trucks.

Swallowing hard, Jake set his mind back on track. The creek bed was dry. If the glut of fallen leaves was anything to go by, it hadn't flooded in months.

There was still the garage to search, he reminded himself—easily a thousand square feet of hiding space.

Yet something held him where he was, as if his feet were rooted to the damp, leaf-strewn earth. Glancing at his watch, he saw that it was past time to check in with Libby. God knows, the last thing she needed was something else to worry about. Discouraged, he turned away.

And then turned slowly back again. That culvert... Something had snagged his attention, but what? Away from the fancy shrubbery and flawlessly manicured lawn immediately surrounding the house, the landscape was already winter bare. Raw red creek bank, thick, damp-barked tree trunks, squirrel-gnawed pine cones littering the carpet of leaves and pine straw, a scrap of yellow yarn...

Yellow yarn!

In three strides, Jake was on his knees, peering into the near end of the culvert. On the sunniest day it might not be hard to see inside, but on a gray afternoon in November, it was damn near impossible!

He called softly. "David? Are you in there, son?"

Nothing. Not a whisper. So why did he feel as if every cell in his body was on full alert?

Something was in there. Hiding. An animal, possibly. A stray dog, looking for a warm place to sleep?

No, a dog would have growled or run out the other end.

Jake figured he had two choices. He could go get Libby and let her try to talk him out, or he could go in after him. If it really was the boy. And with every passing moment, he was more certain that he'd run his quarry to earth.

"Listen, son, you remember what we talked about last weekend out at your uncle's place? Your mama needs you now. She's up at the house, calling all your friends to see if they know where you are. She's worried sick."

No response. Was it only his imagination, or had he heard leaves rustling? Those inside the culvert would probably still be dry enough to rustle.

"David, your mother's come to take you home. You and—uh, Ikky."

This was prime copperhead country. Jake could only hope the recent cold snap had sent them all into hibernation.

"Ikky's losing his hair. Ever think about getting him a helmet?" Jake stretched out on his belly at one end of the culvert, hoping the kid wouldn't slip out the other end. It got dark so damned early these days.... "David? Your

mama's pretty miserable, son. I think it might be a good
idea now to go let her know you're all right.''

Jake's pulses leaped. That had been a definite sniffle
he'd heard. At the sounds of scuffling, he closed his eyes
momentarily and then held out a hand to help the small,
filthy figure crawl the last few feet.

It seemed like days, but it was hardly more than an hour
before they were on their way west again. The policeman
had turned out to be a pretty decent sort. What the hell
could he have said after the boy had told him that he was
only waiting until it was time to go home, that he had
asked and asked his daddy to take him back home, but his
daddy had yelled at him and pinched his neck, and David
had decided to wait outside until it was time to go back
home.

And then there had been Porter to deal with. Jake freely
admitted that might have gone smoother if he hadn't been
there. On the other hand, Libby had needed him. The jerk
would have walked all over her if he hadn't stepped in.

Jake had sent Libby and David upstairs, with Rosa following along to pack his things. Denise hung over Porter's chair, and Jake figured she may as well hear what he
had to say. All he wanted was to get it said and then to get
Libby and her son out of there.

He opened his mouth to let fly a few home truths, when
the bimbo interrupted. ''Sweety, you didn't mean what
you were saying about getting full custody, did you?''

''Keep out of this, Denise,'' Porter snapped.

''But Wally—''

Jake heard Libby coming downstairs. This could get
real ugly, real fast, and dammit, she didn't need this!
''Porter, why do you keep throwing this custody business
around? You know damned well you don't want full cus-

tody, even if you could bribe a judge to give it to you!''
Jake had already figured out that one. The grandmother
was probably loaded, and Porter didn't want to take a
chance on his son's portion going astray.

"Quite frankly, Hatcher, I don't see what business that
is of yours. In fact, I don't see what you're doing here at
all."

"The name's Healy. John Hatcher Healy. And if it
concerns Libby, then it's my business."

Porter's pale eyes had narrowed. Denise made the mistake of popping her gum at that moment, and Porter
slapped her on the fanny and told her to go play with her
jewelry for a while.

Jake waited for the explosion. None came. Instead he
watched in amazement as the lissome lady sauntered down
the hall with every evidence of good humor. He heard her
speak to Libby in the hallway, and he lowered his own
voice. "As to what I'm doing here, Libby wasn't in any
shape to make a two-hour drive. I volunteered."

"Oh, I see," Walt said, a sneer implicit in the comment.

The call had come in just after daybreak that morning.
"I expect you do," Jake said smoothly. "To get back to
this custody thing, if you and Miss Keith are getting married, I suppose you're figuring a court might consider a
two-parent household more suitable than what Libby can
provide, am I right?"

"I think that's between me and my ex-wife."

"Maybe. Or maybe it's between your son and your
girlfriend, I don't know. I do know that it's not going to
work. And I'm warning you, Porter, if you ever—*ever*—
try to play your little mind games with Libby again, for
any reason whatsoever, I'm going to drive you into the

ground. And believe me," he added softly, "I'm looking forward to the pleasure."

Porter's face flushed a dark shade of red. His pale eyes moved over Jake's unshaved countenance, his wrinkled and now muddy clothing. He plucked an invisible thread off the sleeve of his pale blue cashmere sweater. "You're going to marry her yourself, Healy?"

"That's between Libby and me. You threw her away, Porter. She was the best thing that ever happened to you, but you were too stupid to know what you had. I almost feel sorry for you." Hearing the two women in the hallway part company, he added quietly, "If you're smart, you'll marry your lady friend. She's too good for you, but she just might feel sorry enough for you to overlook what you are."

And then, turning to where Libby and David waited with the housekeeper, he said, "If you're ready to ride, honey, let's go home."

David slept in the back seat, securely belted down, his head propped up against the coat Jake had rolled up in the corner. Ikky slept beside him, little worse for the day's adventure.

Jake wondered how David would like a puppy.

With one hand, he rummaged through his cassette holder and pulled out a Brahms from among the Haggard, Jones and Travis. He figured Libby needed some space right now, and a four-door sedan only offered so much of that.

By the time the tape ended, they were almost to Greensboro. Libby switched it off, drew in a deep breath, and turned to him for the first time since they'd pulled out of Porter's driveway. "Thank you, Jake. Not just for finding David, but for—for being there. I don't think I could have handled it if it hadn't been for you."

"You'd have handled it just fine," he told her. If it wasn't for the traffic, the child in the back seat, and the fact that once he made his move, he had no intention of being interrupted, Jake would have pulled over into the emergency lane right then and there and kissed her until neither of them had a rational thought in their heads.

But that, too, would have to wait.

Twelve

By nine-forty-five that night, Libby had broken three of her short fingernails by drumming them on the side table. She had washed every dish in sight, picked up everything that wasn't nailed down, and reread the front page of the *Journal* at least twice without taking in a single word.

And that was after seeing David bathed, fed and bedded down, and getting her own shower. She had put on a sage green velvet hostess gown that had languished forever in the back of her closet, added a dab of eye shadow, a wisp of peach-colored blusher and lip gloss, and then fought against the urge to scrub it all off and change into her oldest jeans.

Oh, heavens, he should have been here by now!

Should she have worn her suede flats instead of her slippers? Bedroom slippers were so...

Maybe he wasn't coming. Maybe he had changed his mind and decided he didn't want to get in any deeper than he already was. She couldn't much blame him.

No, she refused to believe that. "See you later," he'd said. That could mean anything. Later next week. Later this year. Later after David had left for college.

"Oh, bosh," she muttered, and just as she turned away from the front window, a pair of low headlights swept across the front yard. There was a squeal of brakes, the slam of a car door, and Libby opened the front door, swallowing down a sickening surge of sheer panic. She hadn't felt like this since the day of her senior prom, when she'd been still hoping against hope that someone would invite her at the very last minute.

No one had, of course. And after it was all over and she had laid to rest her secret hopes, she had got over it. The same way she would get over this, if she had to.

Did a woman ever grow too old to hope?

Jake's eyes gleamed darkly as he stepped into the living room, his freshly shaved cheeks flushed from the cold. The fingers of his left hand worked over a set of keys, clicking brass against brass. "Sorry to be so late. If you'd rather I left . . ."

"Oh, no, you're not late! I was just getting ready to read the— That is, won't you—um, your coat?"

"Oh. Yeah, sure. Thanks." He shed his leather jacket, his gaze moving over her slender back as she made room for it in the closet.

Damn. Wearing that long velvety thing, she looked like the angel on top of a Christmas tree. He could at least have worn a tie instead of corduroys and a black flannel shirt. Nice going, man. You're really going to impress the hell out of her tonight, aren't you?

"I made fresh coffee. It's coconut-and-chocolate-flavored. I've been saving it for a special occasion."

A special occasion. Was that his cue? Jake felt his palms start to sweat. He hadn't exactly rehearsed it, but he'd gone over what he intended to say a few dozen times while he showered, shaved and dressed. It wasn't every day of the week that a man asked a woman to marry him. The first time had been relatively painless. He and Cass had been lovers for more than a year by then, and her family had been urging them for months to make it legal. Having just seen a new year in, neither of them had been entirely sober on the night he had finally got around to proposing.

Somehow Jake had a feeling coconut-chocolate-flavored coffee wasn't going to help much.

"Come on into the kitchen and I'll see what I can find to go with it. David ate the last of the gingerbread men, but I usually keep an assortment of cookies and crackers on hand for emergencies."

Jake figured this could easily be classed as an emergency. "Speaking of David, is he asleep yet?"

"He was pretty keyed up. I left him looking at treasure-hunting books. Usually he falls asleep with his light on and I go up and turn it off and cover him up."

Ignoring the two cups, the plate of crackers and cheese she had arranged on a tray, Jake said, "I'd like to go up and talk to him if he's still awake—that is, if you don't mind."

Wordlessly Libby shook her head. She couldn't imagine what he had to say to her son, but then, the two of them seemed to have some sort of unspoken understanding ever since they had showed up back at the house earlier that day. From an upstairs window, Libby had watched them walking back up the hill. Jake had looked grim, and David had looked tear-stained, even from that distance. He had been clinging to Ikky with one hand and to Jake with the other.

As Jake headed up the stairs, Libby stood in the middle of the kitchen staring blindly at a childish drawing pinned to the bulletin board. Dear Lord, if five minutes alone with a man affected her this way—drumming pulses, cold sweats, trembling hands—the last thing she needed was caffeine!

"Hello, David. Your mama thought you might be asleep by now," Jake said quietly. The boy was slumped back against the bedstead, arms crossed behind his head, a treasure-hunting magazine open over his chest. Ikky was beside him, carefully tucked under the covers.

"I stay up real late sometimes. Sometimes I stay up all night, longer even than Mama does."

"Yeah, me too. Kinda hard to sleep when a guy's got a lot on his mind."

David appeared to think it over. He shrugged. "Yeah. I guess."

"Sometimes talking things over with a friend helps," Jake suggested.

"Jeffie doesn't know very much about stuff like...you know. Divorce and all. His mama and daddy don't even fight much."

"Well, I'd say Jeffie's a pretty lucky boy, then."

"I guess." David plucked at the dinosaur quilt, and Jake cleared his throat. This wasn't turning out to be quite as easy as he'd thought.

"Are you going to marry my mama?"

Well, that was laying it on the line, all right. "I'll level with you, David. I'd like to marry your mama—I'd like that a whole lot, but not if you've got a problem with it."

Silence. If the kid was deliberately trying to make things tough for him, he was doing a damned fine job of it.

"See, the thing is, I really need your mama, David. Oh, I know—you do, too, but maybe we could sort of work out something."

"I don't know if there's room or not. There's lots of old boxes and stuff in the other bedroom."

"I guess your mama and I could come up with something if we tried hard enough. Maybe we could double up. Like you and Ikky do."

"Maybe. Do you like little boys?"

Jake winced. When he spoke again, his voice was rough, soft, like old burlap. "Yeah, son, I like little boys. I had one of my own once, but he—he died. And you want to know something? It hurts really bad. I guess that's why sometimes I can't get to sleep."

The small figure beside him was still for a long time. Jake wondered what the hell he was doing here, trying to explain to a kid who was too young to understand—hell, he didn't even understand himself. All he knew was that it was important that David understand right from the first that to most men, little boys were infinitely precious. Unique individuals to be loved, to be remembered. To be cherished.

"Maybe I'd let you play with Ikky sometimes," David said tentatively.

"I'd like that."

"I'm too big to play with dolls, but Ikky's still little. That's why I let him sleep with me."

"Yeah, I figured that."

"So if you want to live with Mama and me, I guess that's all right, too."

Jake reached out and then let his arms fall to his sides. He wanted to—he felt like—but dammit, if he pushed too hard, the kid would spook. There'd be plenty of time later. All the time in the world. And this time, Jake would make the most of every rare and precious moment.

"I guess I'd better get back to your mama and ask her how soon I can move in with you guys. My place is pretty lonesome," he said, rising almost reluctantly.

"We have gingerbread a lot, but Mama gets cross sometimes, 'specially when she has a cold. Sometimes her eyes get real red."

"Then we'll just have to take care of her so she won't have so many colds," Jake said. He was almost out the door when David called his name.

"Jake?"

"Yeah, son?"

"Do you have a tank wagon?"

Jake's grin used muscles that hadn't been exercised in more than seven years. "No, but I've got something even better. Meet me here tomorrow after school, and I'll show you."

When Jake came down some quarter of an hour later, he found Libby in the living room on the sofa, the folds of her gown artfully arranged to cover the bare feet she had drawn up beside her. Two lamps had been left on, the harsh overhead light turned off. On the coffee table there was a tray containing a warming carafe, two cups and an assortment of crackers and cheeses.

"Did you eat supper?" he asked.

"I had a bowl of chicken soup with David," she murmured. But Libby wasn't thinking about food. She wanted to know what had passed between this man and her son. Jake looked somehow different, as if a spring that had been wound too tight for too long had finally been released.

He sat down beside her, leaned his head back against the cushion and closed his eyes for a moment, then he began to speak. "There's this old-fashioned custom, you know...something my grandfather mentioned when I was about twelve and just starting to get interested in girls." Opening his eyes, he turned to face her, and Libby's breath caught in her throat.

"A custom?" she repeated, her hand hovering over the carafe.

"Something about asking the man of the house for permission to pay court to one of his womenfolk."

Libby's eyes unexpectedly brimmed with tears as she stared at the ruggedly handsome man who had turned her life upside down in a few short weeks. Who *was* he? John J. Hatcher Healy, socialite, business magnate, rescuer of pregnant strangers at five-hundred-dollar-a-plate fundraisers? Or Jake Hatcher, big-iron man, who drove a muddy pickup truck and ate gingerbread parts in her kitchen and dived into fish ponds after clumsy women?

How could any man who was powerful enough and tough enough to control thousands of tons of heavy metal, be gentle enough to earn the trust of a small, badly frightened child? How could a man who had survived the loss of a child and the breakup of his marriage ever find the strength and courage to start over and build a new life?

Libby was certain of only one thing where Jake Hatcher was concerned. Whoever he was—whatever he was—she loved him through and through—always would, and quite possibly always had.

"So," Jake said after a while, "I asked him."

"You asked—Jake, what are you trying to say?"

"Botching it, huh?"

"That's one way of putting it."

Reaching out, Jake drew her into his arms, arranging her so that she was leaning back against his chest. With his lips buried in the silken fragrance of her hair, he said, "Like I said, I asked him and he said he guessed it would be okay, and then he asked me if I had a tank wagon."

"You asked *who*—"

"I think that's *whom,*" he rumbled softly into her right ear.

"Asked whom *what?*"

Jake chuckled, and the sound resonated all the way to the soles of her feet. "Now you've gone and got me all mixed up. I asked David. As for the what, I asked him if he'd have any objections to my marrying his mama."

Libby swallowed a lungful of air and choked on it. By the time she had recovered, she was sprawled across Jake's lap, and he had somehow managed to get his hand inside her gown to thump her on the back.

"Honey, you're not a whole lot better at this business than I am. You want to cut it short?"

"No, I don't want to cut it short! Cut what short? I want to know what he said, and—and why you even asked, and . . . Jake, *do* you want to marry me?"

"Didn't I just say so?"

Burying her face in his warm throat, Libby let the tears that had been threatening all day spill out. Jake held her. He didn't attempt to talk. He didn't try to soothe her, didn't utter a single there-there. After a while, she sat up and knuckled her red-rimmed eyes. "I m-might as well not have bothered with eye shadow," she muttered. "Jake, I'm sorry. I don't usually cry, but it's been . . ."

"One of those days?" His smile might not have been calculated to render her totally helpless, but it had that effect.

"And nights. Last night, I mean—and then this morning." She dried her face on the hem of her gown. Straightening up, she tried for composure, giving it up as hopeless after the third residual sob. "But don't let me interrupt you. You were saying..."

Jake threw back his head and laughed. "Ah, Libby, how did I ever make it so long without you? You know what you are?"

Half-afraid to ask, she shook her head.

"You're real. You're more than skin-deep, you're Libby clean through. And sweetheart, you don't know how rare and wonderful that is." Slipping his arms around her, he toppled her so that she lay sprawled across him, and with his forehead resting against hers, he whispered, "Fortunately, I do."

* * * * *

A romantic collection that
will touch your heart....

Mother to *with* *Love* '93

Diana Palmer
Debbie Macomber
Judith Duncan

As part of your annual tribute to
motherhood, join three of Silhouette's
best-loved authors as they celebrate the
joy of one of our most precious gifts—
mothers.

Available in May at your favorite retail outlet.

Only from 🔻 *Silhouette*®

—where passion lives.

Take 4 bestselling love stories FREE

Plus get a FREE surprise gift!

SILHOUETTE® Desire®

HAWK'S WAY

HAWK'S WAY—where the Whitelaws of Texas run free till passion brands their hearts. A hot new series from Joan Johnston!

Look for the first of a long line of Texan adventures, beginning in April with THE RANCHER AND THE RUNAWAY BRIDE (D #779), as Tate Whitelaw battles her bossy brothers—and a sexy rancher.

Next, in May, Faron Whitelaw meets his match in THE COWBOY AND THE PRINCESS (D #785).

Finally, in June, Garth Whitelaw shows you just how hot the summer can get in THE WRANGLER AND THE RICH GIRL (D #791).

Join the Whitelaws as they saunter about HAWK'S WAY looking for their perfect mates . . . only from Silhouette Desire!

**Silhouette Books
is proud to present
our best authors,
their best books...
and the best in
your reading pleasure!**

Throughout 1993, look for exciting books
by these top names in contemporary
romance:

CATHERINE COULTER—
Aftershocks in February

FERN MICHAELS—
Nightstar in March

DIANA PALMER—
Heather's Song in March

ELIZABETH LOWELL
Love Song for a Raven in April

SANDRA BROWN
(previously published under
the pseudonym Erin St. Claire)—
Led Astray in April

LINDA HOWARD—
All That Glitters in May

When it comes to passion,
we wrote the book.

Silhouette®

BOBT1RR

Fifty red-blooded, white-hot, true-blue hunks from every State in the Union!

Beginning in May, look for MEN: MADE IN AMERICA! Written by some of our most popular authors, these stories feature fifty of the strongest, sexiest men, each from a different state in the union! Favorite stories by such bestsellers as Debbie Macomber, Jayne Ann Krentz, Mary Lynn Baxter, Barbara Delinsky and many, many more!

Plus, you can receive a FREE gift, just for enjoying these special stories!

You won't be able to resist MEN: MADE IN AMERICA!

Two titles available every other month at your favorite retail outlet.